"**M**a'am...don't!" she protested as I dug it rather hard into her flesh at a precise spot between her buttocks, knowing how she hated the pleasure it gave her to be touched there.

"I shall do exactly as I please," I replied. "And since you are my possession, you will behave exactly as I instruct you to behave. Is that perfectly clear?"

A second jab of the cane was enough to secure a moan of assent from Patsy.

"'Twas only that I didn't want other women seeing my...you know...seeing me there," she protested.

"Hold your tongue, lest you condemn yourself still further."

I contemplated the two backsides presented so beautifully for chastisement. Each was alluring and stimulating in its own way: Indhira's small, rounded cheeks with their skin of caramel-gold, so firm and springy; Patsy's coarser, ampler charms, with their dimpled flesh rippling so invitingly underneath the false modesty of her drawers. Such pleasure could be derived so simply. Ah, but where to begin? That was the tantalizing, intoxicating question.

Also by VALENTINA CILESCU:

BODY & SOUL

MISTRESS WITH A MAID, VOLUME 3

VALENTINA CILESCU

Body and Soul: Mistress With a Maid, Volume 3
Copyright © 1997 by Valentina Cilescu
All Rights Reserved

First Rosebud Edition 1997

First Printing May 1997

ISBN 1-56333-515-8

Manufactured in the United States of America
Published by Masquerade Books, Inc.
801 Second Avenue
New York, N.Y. 10017

CHAPTER 1

From the journal of Dr. Claudia Dungarrow, formerly Fellow of St. Matilda's College, Cambridge:

I felt the cool rush of air caress my body as I walked through the forest. Dry twigs and leaves prickled the undersides of my bare feet. Sharp-tipped branches sprang back to chastise my naked flesh. I purred with contentment to feel the sheer power of my sensual will. How could any woman resist me? Unless, perhaps, that woman were Elizabeth Stanbridge....

My body tensed briefly at the memory of the darling doe-eyed wretch who had betrayed me not once, but again and again. She was no longer my plaything, for we had parted company many months since; yet still she filled my thoughts and peopled my dreams with fantasies of the cruelest and most piquant pleasure.

"Elizabeth," I murmured to myself in the silence of the forest. "You may fly from my embrace, but you are and always will be my creation. You will never know true happiness until you also learn the true ecstasy of obedience."

Lost in thought, at first I did not notice the muffled sounds of revelry filtering between the trees. I stopped and listened. Girlish laughter and half-stifled sighs were coming from a little way ahead. Intrigued, I moved closer to the source of the sound, taking care to conceal my approach.

I was rewarded by the sight of the prettiest tête-à-tête imaginable. In a small clearing beside a woodland stream were two girls of seventeen or eighteen. One was long-limbed and slender, with ash-blonde hair which tumbled untidily over the small, pale breasts peeping through her unbuttoned blouse. She was kneeling over her companion, a dark-haired girl, smaller in stature but more womanly in form.

This darker nymph was almost naked, her blue skirt, white blouse and knee-length bloomers cast aside on the grass, leaving her clad only in white silk stockings and tight-laced stays, over which her mountainous breasts tumbled with a sluttish readiness which made me thirst to taste them on my tongue.

She lay on her back on the grass, her thighs parted to

reveal the dark triangle of her maidenhair and the luscious mouth of her sex, pouting coquettishly between her silky thighs.

I stroked my hand lightly over my own breast, feeling the nipple harden almost instantly at the faint touch. Moist warmth oozed most agreeably between my thighs, and I squeezed them together, relishing the gentle throbbing sensation from my swollen clitoris. How delightful to come upon such an unexpectedly erotic entertainment. Laying my cheek against the bark of a tree, I settled myself to watch and listen....

"Maddie," giggled the dark-haired girl, "you mustn't!"

She wriggled like an eel as her companion stooped over her and insinuated her tongue tip between her breasts. The blonde girl emerged red-faced and panting.

"Oh, but Caro, you know I must." She sighed. "Your titties taste so wonderful..."

"But what if someone were to find us here? Miss Sanderson...or one of the chaperones...?"

Maddie responded by stripping off her frilly white blouse and tossing it carelessly onto the ground.

"My dear Caro, I couldn't care less!"

She reached behind her and unbuttoned her skirt, letting it fall to the ground, gliding over the smooth white globes of her buttocks. Ah, how delectably kissable they were beneath her gauzy bloomers, split generously at the crotch—no doubt for reasons of hygiene, but so very stimulating to the observer; her split fig oozing juice through the gaping slit in the cotton lawn.

"There!" declared Maddie. "Now I am as naked as you."

"Except for your bloomers," chided Caro.

"If you would have them off, you must take them off yourself," teased Maddie. "With your teeth," she added naughtily.

I watched with a mixture of amusement and lustful expectation as Maddie urged Caro to kneel before her and take down her bloomers with her teeth, easing and tugging down the fabric inch by inch, revealing ever-more-tantalizing glimpses of girlish flesh. What potential, I thought to myself. As yet almost untapped, it was true, and certainly in need of the proper discipline; but tanta-lizing in its glittering depths.

At last the bloomers yielded with the faintest whisper, floating down Maddie's long limbs like a flimsy white cloud. She stepped out of them and stood imperiously before her friend, a sprinkling of dusky-blonde curls scarcely veiling the plump juiciness of her pubescent sex. Lovingly, yet rather haughtily, she laid her hands on Caro's head and began stroking her hair.

"Do you find me...pleasing?" she whispered.

"Oh, yes!"

"More pleasing than"—she considered—"than Antoine DuClos?"

At this, Caro let out a little shriek of scandalized laughter.

"Monsieur DuClos? The fencing master? Oh Maddie, how could you even begin to imagine…!"

Maddie's index finger played idly down Caro's cheek and teased the plump pink rosebud of her mouth.

"You have never thought…what it might be like to have him fuck you?"

"Maddie! Maddie, I swear—"

"You wouldn't want him to take out his dick and put it inside you? Or the young lieutenant to slip his hand inside your chemise and squeeze your titties…?"

As she spoke, Maddie slid her hands underneath Caro's breasts and lifted them out, pressing them gently together so that the nipples nestled against each other like the tiny pink muzzles of newborn kittens.

"Oh. Oh, Maddie!" Caro groaned as Maddie's thumbs flicked lightly over her swollen nipples. "Oh, Maddie, don't torture me so! You know I could never… not with a man. The very thought disgusts me!"

"Do you know what I should like?" Maddie whispered wickedly. Caro raised her eyes; they were round and attentive. It was obvious to me that she found this game every bit as compelling as her companion.

"What, Maddie?"

"I should like to be Claudia Dungarrow."

"No!" Caro gasped, but I knew from the trembling of her whole body that she found more than a little favor in the idea.

"And if I were Claudia, I should like to ravish you, my

9

darling Caro. Wouldn't you like that, my dearest, to be ravished by the great and beautiful Claudia Dungarrow?"

Caro closed her eyes and I heard her exhale, very slowly.

"Yes," she whispered. "Oh, she is so…so powerful. If only I could have her hands on me. If just once I could be her favorite. Feel her tongue on my bare skin…"

Maddie massaged Caro's breasts, rubbing and caressing her nipples, fueling her forbidden fantasies.

"Tell me," she urged. "Tell me what you would have Mistress Dungarrow do to you."

"I…it is a hot summer night… I am walking home alone. I hear footsteps.…"

"It is Mistress Claudia?"

Caro nodded.

"She steps out onto the path before me. She is dressed all in black, a beautiful dress of black silk that swishes about her ankles…and shiny red boots with high heels…and the dress is cut very low in the bodice, I can almost see her nipples…"

"Tell me what she does to you, Caro."

I smiled to myself as I watched this little pantomime. Before Caro even opened her mouth, I knew precisely what she would say; though admittedly alluring, the fluffy-headed child was lamentably predictable in her desires.

"She has a riding crop. She strikes me across the cheek with it and tells me I have been very wicked. I fall to the ground, sobbing, and she is standing over me—"

Caro let out a squeal of surprise and pleasure as Maddie lunged forward and pushed her to the ground.

"You are an extremely wicked girl," Caro purred, in a girlish parody of my voice. "And I simply will not tolerate disobedience. I shall have to punish you."

"And then," sighed Caro, still sunk deep in her fantasy, "then she whips me until my clothes are in tatters, and I am struggling and crying out, but secretly all I am feeling is perfect ecstasy...."

Maddie knelt over Caro, her outspread thighs forming a pointed arch that cast a shadow across her face.

"And then, my dearest? And then what next?" Her thighs tensed about Caro's body, the moist triangle of her sex sparkling with unshed tears of desire.

"She...pins me to the ground...and kneels over me. And she lifts up her skirts..."

"Go on. Tell me."

"Underneath she is naked. And her pussy is all shaven. Can you imagine it—smooth and gaping wide? I can see the hard stalk of her clitty, pushing out like a little pink tongue."

"And what does Claudia make you do?"

"She pushes her pussy into my face and tells me I must drink her juices. I breathe in her scent, and it's so very, very sweet I just can't resist...."

I almost laughed out loud as Maddie lowered herself onto Caro's face, her thighs flexing supply and her labia pouting wide in an insistent kiss. These two

11

impetuous girls were displaying rather more lust than skill, but their enthusiasm was an education in itself.

"Lick me out, slut!" Maddie commanded. And the slut thrust her eager tongue deep into the dark haven of her friend's sweet young quim. I smiled.

Such a natural aptitude deserved to be recognized— and taken full advantage of.

Lately I have been working extremely hard on my new treatise, *Dominance and Submission: Aspects of Sapphic Love*, and it has been my practice to breakfast early and write until noon, take a nap, then rise refreshed and attend to the education of my Sapphic Circle.

The day after the incident in the forest, I was delighted to find an excellent attendance at my afternoon instructional lecture. These occasional lectures have acquired a certain social cachet among ladies of quality, and there are many who have been persuaded to the ways of Sapphic pleasure through the beauties of rational argument alone—though I confess that others are drawn by the power of my own sensuality, and the cruel beauty of the whip.

I dressed carefully, in a gown of black-trimmed crimson, with elbow-length gloves of fine black leather and patent-leather boots laced to the knee. Contemplating myself somewhat critically in the mirror, I turned to my faithful maid Patsy.

"The gold jewelry or the jet?"

"The jet is very fine, madam."

"Yes. You are quite right. Give me the bracelet and the collar. This afternoon I wish to be certain of ensuring the proper impact."

Patsy fastened the collar about my neck and I viewed the transformation approvingly. A triple collar of heavy black jet beads caressed my bare throat; and from it, suspended on the finest silver chain, hung a carved oval, on which was carved the image of two naked women, entwined sensually. Nestling in the deep valley of my décolletage, it made a pretty picture.

Securing my veiled hat with a diamond pin, I went outside. My ladies were already gathered in the large, well-tended garden at the back of the Hall, taking a genteel afternoon tea on the lawns. My guests numbered over a dozen, and ranged from venerable matrons like Henrietta Lowndes and the Colonel's wife, to the beautiful, tomboyish Ursula Maryland.

And there, giggling and simpering like a pair of over-grown schoolgirls, were the two wood nymphs I had caught sight of in the forest: wide-eyed Caro and her wanton friend Maddie. How very different they seemed from the last time I had seen them, now so girlish and virginal in their matching dresses of pale lemon muslin, the very epitome of unsullied English womanhood.

Would they greet me so artlessly, I wondered, if they knew that I had witnessed their woodland frolics? In any event, it was perfectly plain from their childish and uncontrolled behavior that these two jades were in urgent need of lessons in discipline.

I gathered my ladies about me and began my lecture. How they hung on my every word, enraptured by the hidden violence of my sensuality, glimpsed so tantalizingly beneath my outward veneer of cool detachment. How easy it was to play them like fish on my line.

"The essence of all pleasure," I announced, "is self-control."

Puzzled glances ran round the circle. Then Ursula Maryland voiced their doubts.

"Mistress? How can that be? Is not self-abandonment the very essence of all pleasure?"

"On the contrary," I replied. "In order for pleasure to be more than a brief spark, in order for it to endure, it must be allied to the strictest sense of discipline."

"But Mistress Claudia…what form must this discipline take?"

"Every form. You must make it the cornerstone of your whole life." I allowed my gaze to wander over the upturned, expectant faces. "Perhaps I should explain in simpler terms. Women are divided into two kinds: those who are born to dominate, and those who are born to serve."

"Then there may be no truly equal partnerships between women?" inquired the Colonel's wife with some consternation.

"Naturally there may: in simple comradeship. And all

sensual partnerships are complementary, for dominance and submission naturally complement each other. But if order and happiness are to result, the submissive must always relinquish her will to that of her dominatrix."

"Why should this be?" demanded Henrietta Lowndes, evidently alarmed by the prospect of being considered a mere submissive, incapable of choosing her own sensual path.

"Because only her dominatrix truly understands her needs."

"But how can she? Surely—"

I raised my hand and silence prevailed.

"The dominatrix offers firmness and discipline, instilling that sense of control without which the submissive can not hope to ascend to the summit of purest pleasure. And furthermore"—I smiled back at Henrietta—"it is only through selfless pleasure-giving and the abdication of her own desires that the submissive can attain that level of pleasure. That is the plain truth of the feminine condition."

Ripples of excitement ran through the assembled women. I knew from their flushed faces and excited whispers that Caro and Maddie were particularly impressed by what I had said. They were so lost in their own conversation that they did not notice me step forward and make my way toward them.

In point of fact, it was not until I cast a shadow across their faces that Maddie looked up, nudging Caro's arm so that she, too, turned her round dove-grey eyes on me.

"Oh, Dr. Dungarrow! We were just—"

"What wicked girls you are."

No smile was permitted to cross my face. I was implacable, my pleasure rooted in Maddie's confusion and Caro's absolute discomfiture. If Maddie cherished ambitions of becoming a dominatrix, she must first understand and experience the joys of submission.

"Mistress?"

"You are a wicked girl, Maddie. Wicked and disobedient. I cannot tolerate disobedience, and so I shall have to punish you. Shan't I?"

I slid the riding crop from my belt and stroked its flexible tip between my fingers. The silver filigree decoration caught the light and Maddie's soft brown eyes fixed upon it, mesmerized by what she knew instinctively was to come. Was she wondering, perhaps, how I had guessed the exact composition of her most potent sexual fantasy, to the extent of echoing her own words?

"Shan't I, Maddie?"

The brown eyes met mine, and the tip of Maddie's tongue flicked nervously across her parched lips.

"Oh, yes, Mistress."

From the journal of Miss Elizabeth Stanbridge:
Will this torment never end?

It is now many months since I left the household of Claudia Dungarrow, and came to Milnrow House as private tutor to Lady Fallowfield's daughter. I came here with the intention of leaving behind my former life forever, escaping from the many varieties of sensual corruption which had been instilled in me by my wicked mentor, but Claudia's words and deeds and caresses live on in my every waking thought, my every dream, and I begin to believe that I shall never be truly free.

When first Demelza Fitzgerald and I were abducted by Claudia, we were little more than innocent children, happy in our innocent sisterly love—but alas! we were quickly and easily corrupted, and almost effortlessly initiated into the paths of pain, servitude and erotic depravity. How can I ever hope to escape, when I am but what Claudia's desires —and my own depraved aptitudes —have made me?

But no. I will resist. I must.

This afternoon was particularly painful for me. Every afternoon I must spend alone with the Honourable Phoebe Milnrow, Lady Fallowfield's daughter, listening to her practicing the pianoforte. She is an apt pupil, and it is scarcely an onerous duty to listen to Chopin and Liszt études, skillfully executed. But Phoebe is also a deliciously attractive eighteen-year-old girl, young and fresh and just awakening to the demands of her delightful body.

I know full well the thoughts that are passing through that virginal mind. I have seen the look in those midnight-dark eyes, that peep up at me so winsomely from underneath a long sweep of black lashes. She longs for me as I long for her; her body aches with the need to be taken and devoured....

"Miss Elizabeth." She paused in her playing and half-turned toward me, a dark kiss-curl falling prettily over her cheek.

"Yes, Phoebe?"

"This phrase here." She ran her fingertip along the musical stave. I was forced to step nearer in order to see where she was pointing; all too near, for the lavender and honey scents of her body filled my brain until I reeled from the desperate need to touch her.

I forced my voice to remain steady. "What of it?"

"What does *'appassionato e lusingando'* mean?"

"It means..." I cleared my throat, which had suddenly become unaccountably dry. "It means 'passionate and coaxing.'"

"But I don't understand how..."

Her eyes appealed to me, beseeching me with their unspoken message: 'Take me—why won't you take me? Don't you want me? Don't you find me pleasing to your senses? I want you, Miss Elizabeth, I want you to possess me, I'll do anything you command me to. Anything...'

"Here. Let me show you." I slid onto the piano stool, next to her, and executed the phrase. "Now you try."

She tried it twice, but it was still not quite right, so I was forced to lay my hands on hers and move her fingers on the keys while I counted out the beats of the bar in time to the metronome.

"There, Phoebe—do you see now?"

Her eyes would not let me go. They were more

passionate and coaxing than anything I could imagine.

"Oh, yes, Miss Elizabeth. I do so love having you as my teacher."

"Yes…well, I—"

"Do you like teaching me? Do you like me, too, Miss Elizabeth?"

I opened my mouth, but no sound came out. Like her? She could not possibly know how much. My clitoris burned; my breasts ached; my whole body screamed out for release whenever I was in the same room as this pretty morsel of a girl. It was a suffocatingly hot, oppressive afternoon, and I could feel sweat trickling down between my shoulder blades and breasts, making my clothes stick to me. I longed for the freedom of nakedness, and the liberation of all my darkest animal desires.

"Phoebe, of course I like you, but—"

To my immense relief, at that very moment the parlor clock struck four o'clock.

"There, Phoebe, lessons are over for today. Off you go now."

"But couldn't I stay here with you?"

"Hurry now, Phoebe. Your mother is waiting for you in the drawing room."

Whether or not that was true, I neither knew nor cared. All I knew for certain was that I could not risk being in the same room as pretty Phoebe Milnrow one moment longer. As I watched her lithe, slender form skipping away down the hallway to the drawing room, the most dark and shameful fantasies entered my thoughts. Phoebe bound and gagged. Phoebe naked and whipped soundly. Phoebe with her thighs spread, and the juices of her spendings trickling onto my fingers.

How easy it would be. The easiest thing in the world to seduce little Phoebe, enslave her and enjoy her to the full. How easy it would be to become Claudia Dungarrow.

And I must never let that happen.

CHAPTER 2

From the journal of Elizabeth Stanbridge:
I am allowed one half-day's holiday each week, plus one
full day per month—a generous allocation by my
employer, since my duties vis-à-vis her daughter are by
no means excessively taxing.

I awaited today with some impatience, for I had agreed
to meet Demelza at a secluded country inn a few miles
outside Cambridge. Since we broke with Claudia Dungarrow and left to pursue our own lives, Demelza Fitzgerald
and I have grown very close. Nevertheless, we have judged
it wise to conduct our passion discreetly and have declared
ourselves free to pursue other liaisons and flirtations.

It was with a happy heart that I arrived at the inn,

sending my mistress's carriage away with instructions to return in a few hours' time. The weather was fine and warm, with a mellow sunshine which turned the old stones to honey gold.

"A'ternoon, Miss Stanbridge." The innkeeper's younger sister greeted me with a conspiratorial smile, and a lightly bobbed curtsy.

"Good afternoon, Lorna. Is my...friend here?"

"No, miss. She a'n't arrived yet." The girl twirled a lock of hair absentmindedly round her finger. She was a comely wench, very slender in the waist but with womanly breasts and hips that did credit even to that drab brown dress and apron.

"The room is prepared?"

"Just as you like it, miss." The hazel eyes dared an inquisitive peep at me. There was a faint pink blush on her peach-soft cheeks. "You'll be wantin' summat t'eat up there, then?"

I shook my head.

"It's such a lovely day. I shall wait in the garden. Please bring me a pitcher of lemonade and some glasses. I shall eat later, when Miss Fitzgerald arrives."

"As you wish, miss."

She bobbed another, rather ungainly curtsy, which had the agreeable effect of making her large and mobile breasts jiggle beneath her apron. I confess that, after many days of abstinence made all the more unbearable by the constant proximity of Phoebe Milnrow, my sensual needs had reached a peak of intensity. Had it not been for the imminent arrival of my lover Demelza, I might well have yielded to temptation, for the innkeeper's sister was a tasty morsel indeed.

The garden of the inn was a picture of English charm, a riot of cranesbill, lobelia, anemones and hollyhocks. I sat myself down at a table, tucked away in the angle of a mossy wall, and glanced at my pocket-watch.

A quarter to one? How strange. We had arranged to meet at half-past twelve, and Demelza was never late. Still, perhaps some perfectly innocent event had delayed her. In any case, my train of thought was promptly interrupted by the return of the serving girl, an earthenware jug clinking against two glasses on a wooden tray.

"'Ere you are, miss."

"Thank you." My fingers brushed hers briefly as she set the glasses on the table, and this time the girl blushed to the roots of her sandy hair. I slipped a shilling into her hand. "Take this for your trouble."

"Thank you, miss, I'm sure."

"Won't you stay and keep me company?"

"Oh, miss, I couldn't!"

I glanced around the garden. It was virtually empty.

"You're not busy—surely you could spare a few minutes to sit and talk with me…and take a glass of lemonade?"

Lorna hesitated. I could see duty and desire battling for supremacy in her pretty head.

23

"I don't rightly know as I should, miss." She smiled nervously. "But perhaps…just half a glass."

"Just one." I poured Lorna a glass of lemonade and watched her drink it, her smooth skin quivering as the cold liquid trickled down her throat.

"I mustn't be gone long, mind. Barney…he don't like me talkin' with the customers, see. Says I'm lazy."

"I'm sure your brother won't mind. Just this once."

I sat back and contemplated the adorable Lorna. She was, to be honest, not really the sort of girl who would generally appeal to my sensual tastes, but the warm sunshine and the tormenting desire to ease the burning hunger between my thighs lent her an irresistible glamour.

"Tell me, Lorna. Do you like men?"

Lorna cast down her eyes.

"No, miss. Nasty, rough brutes they are."

"You haven't a sweetheart?"

"No. Well…" The deepening blush had turned her face almost crimson. "Oh, miss, I can't say.…"

It did not take much effort to divine her happy secret, and I clapped my hands together in delight.

"Oh, Lorna, sweet girl! You have a sweetheart."

"Hush, miss! Someone will hear."

"Is she pretty, Lorna?"

Lorna paused.

"Yes," she whispered.

"Very pretty?"

"Oh, yes! And so sweet-natured, and lovin', and when she kisses me—oh, miss…"

"I am delighted for you, Lorna, truly I am."

I was about to ask what the dreadful Barney thought about his younger sister's *affaire de coeur* when the back door of the inn was flung open and I saw my darling Demelza rush out into the garden. Her sandy hair was in disarray, one sleeve of her dress bore a tear and her hazel eyes were pink and swollen from weeping.

"Demelza!" I cried, leaping to my feet. "Whatever has happened to you?"

Seeing the look which passed between me and my lover, poor Lorna scuttled away like a frightened rabbit, shutting the door firmly behind her.

"Oh, Elizabeth!" sobbed Demelza, sinking down into the chair which Lorna had vacated. "Oh, Elizabeth, whatever am I going to do?"

I sat down beside her and took her little lace-gloved hand in mine, planting a tender kiss on her cheek.

"Demelza, darling Demelza," I murmured, smoothing my hand over the disordered waves of her hair. "Surely nothing can be so terrible?"

Demelza dabbed at her eyes with an handkerchief, her small bosom rising and falling jerkily with the effort of controlling her sobs. Her full lips quivered with emotion.

"It is Annabella. She…she…"

Heart thumping, I took both her hands in mine and forced her to look into my eyes.

"Tell me. Everything."

"Annabella…has promised my hand to…to another."

Fingers of cold horror ran up and down my spine.

"To a man? Heaven forbid that such a thing should happen!"

Demelza shook her head. "No, not that. To a woman. To someone she wishes to curry favor with. You know how desperately Annabella wishes to regain her high station in society."

"Promised you, Demelza? Sold you like a slave? She cannot!"

"She can, Elizabeth, and she has! And oh, my dear Lizzie, if only you knew how dreadful it all is. This woman—"

"Who is she?"

"Lady Maria Owens. And she…she disgusts me. She is at least sixty years old, with grey hair and a great fat body, like a horrible white slug."

"I tell you, Demelza, she cannot do this to you!" I thumped the table with my clenched fist, anger surging in my breast. "I will not let her. I will not allow this!"

"But Elizabeth, what can you do? My sister has made up her mind; it is all arranged."

It took a huge effort of will to master my rage, transforming it to cold fury.

"Then Lady Annabella Fitzgerald will have to make alternative arrangements," I hissed.

"Elizabeth—you mustn't! You won't do anything foolish—promise me you won't?"

Gently but firmly, I lifted Demelza's hand from my arm.

"I will do whatever I have to do."

The following day, I traveled across country to confront Lady Annabella Fitzgerald.

She and I had been deadly enemies in the days when I was Claudia Dungarrow's slave; so it was perhaps not surprising when her servant returned my calling card with a brusque "Lady Annabella says to tell you she is not at home."

"Not at home!" I pushed the servant to one side. "Then let her tell it to my face."

"Miss, please—"

"Out of my way—or would you have me strike you?" I raised my hand and she flinched. "Now. Where is she?"

"In her study, Madam, but you mustn't…"

I paid her no heed and set off up the stairs with the servant in ineffectual pursuit.

I knew my way around Annabella's house as though it were my own, and went directly to the first-floor drawing room which Annabella had transformed into a study. This was where she received her most valued guests, entertaining them with intimate soirees of Sapphic literature, music and intellectual debate. And indeed, as I approached the door, I heard the faint sounds of quiet conversation, laughter, soft music….

Without knocking, I twisted the handle and flung open the door. Oh, such a delightful scene met my eyes! There was Annabella Fitzgerald, laying a riding crop across the bare backside of a milkmaid, her coarse drawers round her ankles and her skirt tucked into her belt. The girl was leaning forward against the mantelpiece, sighing and moaning as the whip bit into her large, plump backside, leaving a crisscross pattern of interlacing red welts.

Seated around in a semi-circle, like spectators at some theatrical presentation, were three of Annabella's society friends: two young ladies of fashion—sisters, to judge by their almost-identical dress—and an older woman, very fat and unappealing, whom I took to be the dread Maria Owens.

At my dramatic entrance, everything stopped and all eyes turned on me—even the milkmaid gave off moaning and screwed her head round to stare at me with eyes as round as cheddar cheeses.

"What the—!" exclaimed one of the young ladies, leaping to her feet and buttoning her blouse hastily.

"Dear Heaven!" gasped her sister, while Maria Owens lumbered slowly to her feet, a look of utter horror on her face.

"What is this outrage?" she demanded. "Who is this person?"

Annabella said nothing. I stepped into the room.

"Lost your tongue, Annabella? Or has time taught you to regard me with respect?"

At this, Annabella laughed sarcastically.

"Respect, Elizabeth? Respect has to be earned. The only feeling you inspire in me is contempt."

"And what about Demelza? Did you respect her when you sold her off like a slab of meat?"

At this, a flicker of consternation crossed Annabella's haughty, beautiful face.

"Please ladies, if you would retire to the drawing room…for a few moments only."

"Shall I summon assistance, Annabella?" Lady Maria demanded.

"Heavens, no. I shall deal with this…person myself."

Once alone, we glared at each other across the empty study.

"I do not recall inviting you to come here," Annabella sniffed.

"Evidently not," I retorted. "And I would not have come if you had. Indeed, I would not willingly set foot in this house were it not for poor darling Demelza."

"Demelza!" scoffed Annabella. "I might have guessed this would be that silly child's doing. The girl hasn't a single grain of sense in her fluffy little head."

Anger boiled within me. I advanced toward Annabella.

"How dare you treat her so!"

"And how dare you meddle in matters which are none of your concern."

"You have given her hand to a woman who disgusts her!"

29

"I have chosen an excellent match for my sister. In time she will be grateful to me for safeguarding her best interests."

"How can you speak of her best interests? When all you care about is using her to make influential friends. And you have the temerity to describe this as an 'excellent match'?"

Annabella regarded me with an icy stare.

"In my opinion," she spat, "any match is an excellent one if it distances my sister from any intimacy with you."

"And what is that supposed to mean?"

"It means, Elizabeth, that I do not wish my sister to be seen consorting with the sort of filth that even Claudia Dungarrow discards."

"You foulmouthed bitch!"

Rage overtook me with such violence that I flew at Annabella, scratching and clawing at her face and drawing drops of blood on her cheek and neck.

"Poisonous little doxy!" she countered, seizing me by the shoulders and flinging me away from her. She caught me off-balance, and I fell sidelong across the daybed, winded and momentarily helpless.

She sprang on me, throwing me onto my back and crushing me with her knee on my chest. I fought back, kicking out and catching her with my foot in her belly. She fell backward and I leapt after her, cursing her and pummeling her with my fists.

30

Her fingers wound into the fabric of my dress, and as we struggled I felt it tear, exposing my shoulder and one pink-tipped breast. Annabella seized her opportunity to humiliate me by lunging at me and sinking her teeth into my flesh, making me shriek with pain and anger.

"How dare you—how dare you bite me!"

We rolled over and over on the floor, the force of my rage lending me resilience against Annabella's superior strength. But Annabella was altogether taller and more powerfully built, and it was perhaps inevitable that she would gain the upper hand. I swore and bit, kicked and scratched, but she succeeded in seizing me by the hair and rolling me onto my back, straddling me there beneath her like a fly on a pin.

Her perfume was sickly-sweet in my nostrils, overlaying the potent scent of our mingled sweat. And in spite of myself, I felt my pulse race, my whole body tingling at the instinctive anticipation of what was about to happen to me.

"Little guttersnipe," hissed Annabella. "It is high time someone taught you a lesson you will never forget."

The next thing I knew, she was throwing up my skirts and forcing apart my thighs. The split crotch of my bloomers—a fashion long ago acquired from my Mistress Claudia—displayed the fruits of my sex with helpless immodesty, leaving me quite unable to resist Annabella's foul intent.

"You shall not touch me!" I snarled, but already her

31

fingers were between the lips of my sex and something else—something cold and hard and huge—was following, ramming its way hard into the shamefully wet heart of me.

With horror I realized what it was: the plaster statuette of Sappho which had stood upon the library table by the door. Annabella had had it in her hand as we fought; no doubt her intention had been to strike me with it, but another, more lascivious thought had entered her mind.

"No!" I shrieked, but it was too late. Already she was possessing me, forcing me to acknowledge not only her superior strength, but the power of my own sensual desires.

Denial had built up a terrible wellspring of need within me, and at the first touch of Annabella's violating fingers on my too-long-denied sex, I felt the sweet, soft ooze of longing trickle between my labia as though at the kiss of a lover. I heard her laugh as I wept tears of humiliation and lust.

"Stupid, headstrong slut. Have you not one ounce of self-control?"

It might almost have been the voice of Claudia Dungarrow.

It was late when I returned to Milnrow Hall, burning with the humiliation and anger of being fucked and discarded by Lady Annabella Fitzgerald. Not only that,

but stripped and thrown out onto the street, with a
warning never to return—unless, of course, I wished for
more of the selfsame treatment.

Fortunately, one of Annabella's maids had always
held a torch for me, and she assisted me in obtaining
fresh clothes—otherwise I should indeed have presented
a sorry sight at the gates of Milnrow Hall.

If I had hoped to slip in unnoticed, I was quickly
disappointed. My heart skipped a beat as I turned my
key in the lock of the servants' entrance and the door
swung open, revealing a solitary figure dozing at the
kitchen table.

"Phoebe! What on earth are you doing here?"

The girl skipped up at the sound of my voice, her
soft brown eyes instantly banishing all thought of sleep.

"Oh, Miss Elizabeth! You have returned at last! I was
beginning to think you had deserted us."

"Why on earth would I do that?" I demanded, half-
irritated and half-excited by this unexpected welcoming
party. There was no denying the allure of young Phoebe
Milnrow, so obviously naked beneath that chaste nightdress of crisply laundered cotton.

"I do not know, but...but I thought perhaps I had
done something to displease you." She swallowed. "And
I want so much to please you, Miss Elizabeth. More than
anything else in the world."

I cannot deny that what I did next was more out of a
spirit of vengeance than of tender affection. Annabella's

violation and humiliation of me had left me burning with the need to rediscover my own sensual potency. And oh! how potent was my desire to taste that sweet, honey-scented, undefiled body which was offering itself to me without the slightest understanding of what it was doing.

"You truly wish to please me?" I whispered, drawing the girl closer to me and softly closing the kitchen door against any intrusion.

"Oh, yes, Miss."

"And you wish me to awaken you to the pleasures of your own womanhood?"

She mouthed "yes," but I knew that she understood nothing of what I had said, only the irresistible waves of need that were pulsing through her youthful body. Phoebe Milnrow trusted me utterly, and that night I took the fullest possible advantage of that trust.

Swiftly but tenderly, I undressed her, unbuttoning her nightdress and letting it slip to the ground. Now she was completely naked before me, her long hair freshly brushed and falling in glossy tendrils over perfect shoulders and tiny budding breasts. Her body was scarcely more developed than a child's, her hips still slender and her sex scarcely veiled by a sparse growth of darkly curling hair.

"Part your thighs for me, child."

She obeyed without question, her only sound a soft "oh" of astonishment as my fingers slipped between her

34

legs and sought out the lusciously wet heart of her sex. How she trembled as my fingertip glanced over the bursting bud of her clitoris, so hard and swollen with the need to be stroked and kissed and bitten.

I, too, sighed with pleasure as I took Phoebe's nipple into my mouth, knowing that I was the very first to taste the sweet hardness of her flesh, the first to slide my finger into the superb tightness of her virgin quim.

"Oh! Oh, Miss Elizabeth, please…please don't hurt me!" she murmured. But even as she protested her fear, her love-juice was cascading over my fingers. And a moment later, as I took her nipple between my teeth and bit the flesh gently, she climaxed, her whole body shuddering as she collapsed forward onto my shoulder, sobbing with ecstasy.

"Oh, Miss Elizabeth!" she breathed, her bosom heaving as she showered my face and neck with grateful kisses. "Thank you, oh, thank you! I never dreamed such pleasure could exist."

"Hush, Phoebe, it has only just begun," I replied, and sliding my hands underneath her wonderfully firm arsecheeks, I lifted her up onto the well-scrubbed kitchen table. With her thighs spread wide, her sex gaped invitingly, the hard stalk of her clit and the tiny, dark mouth of her still-virgin hole distinct and alluring in the flickering candlelight. "I have frigged you, now I am going to fuck you."

"But…but I don't understand," she murmured as I

reached out and picked up a long, thick-handled wooden spoon.

"Trust me," I breathed, and I began sliding the handle of the wooden spoon deep into the tightness of her sex, stifling her cries with kisses as, with a final thrust, I broke through her defenses. "I shall teach you to feel the greatest pleasures any woman can give to another."

CHAPTER 3

From the journal of Claudia Dungarrow:
I have waited too long. Exile is beginning to hang heavy on me, and I grow bored with my life of easy idleness. It is high time that I returned to England and reclaimed what is rightfully mine.

This morning, I instructed my maid Patsy to commence preparations for a long journey. She greeted this news openmouthed with ecstasy.

"Oh, madam! We are to leave this godforsaken country at last?"

I laughed to see the expression of rapture on her face. Foreign climes have not, I fear, agreed with the dear slattern, though I swear she has the constitution of an ox.

"It would appear so," I replied with deliberate coolness.

"Are we returning to England?"

"Perhaps." It amuses me so to tease Patsy. She is as easily manipulated as a half-wit child.

"And we shan't ever have to come back here?" Patsy's desperate hope hung in the air for several seconds before I bothered to reply.

"Get about your duties," I snapped. "And take care that you do not ask too many foolish questions."

Patsy's face fell, and her lower lip jutted sulkily.

"What would you have me do?" she demanded, her tone almost defiant. I chose to ignore her reprehensible behavior—this time. Patsy has done me excellent and faithful service over the years; and when all is said and done, she cannot help being an ignorant peasant.

"Bring Indhira and have the large trunks sent up."

"Yes, ma'am." She turned on her heel with the most insolent curtsy imaginable, and disappeared down the stairs, in search of the Indian maid.

In due course she returned with Indhira, and porters carrying the empty travelling boxes. The Indian girl is a recent acquisition, and a most delightful diversion, with her great dark doe eyes and her glossy black plait, braided with silver thread and swishing like a mare's tail between her supple buttocks. And such an aptitude for submission...

She threw me a shy glance as she entered the room.

"Mistress."

"You are late, Indhira."

"I am sorry, Mistress. I was busy with the laundry."

"When I summon you, you will come instantly. Is that clear?"

"Yes, Mistress." Her eyes seemed to beg, "Punish me, sweet Mistress, I have been such a wicked girl." But menials must learn that I will not inflict pain upon them simply to satisfy their lustful whims.

"I am going on a long journey. To England."

"England, Mistress!"

"You have dreamed of it, slut? Of Buckingham Palace, and riding in Rotten Row in the finest silk and velvet?"

The delightful rosebud mouth formed precisely the right reply: "I dream only of pleasing you, Mistress."

I allowed myself the faintest ghost of a smile. Perhaps the girl was not quite as artless as she appeared. True, she was awkward, naïve and, at times, irritating. But if properly trained, she might be a positive asset on a long and uninteresting voyage.

"You may begin packing. And make sure that you do it properly."

I busied myself with an inventory of my possessions as Patsy fussed and bossed, and Indhira stumbled in her haste to please.

"Take care with that, you stupid girl!" Patsy snapped, fetching Indhira a swipe across the cheek. "That belongs to your Mistress—do you want to feel the weight of her hand as well as mine?" Tears started in Indhira's eyes, but she blinked them back.

"I—I am sorry, I did not mean…"

Patsy gave an exasperated grunt, and picked up the pile of folded chemises which Indhira had dropped.

Indhira's clumsiness increased in proportion to her nervousness. And the girl became more and more nervous with every shout and pinch and slap Patsy gave her.

"Don't you touch those—give them here, you'll only break them."

"I won't!"

"You will. Give them here—you're not fit to serve a proper lady, not like a proper English servant."

I caught my breath as Indhira almost let slip a box filled with tiny bottles fashioned from colored Venetian glass. Patsy snatched them away at the last moment, and packed them in the trunk, making very sure that I saw how much care she was taking not to break any of them.

"That girl's an idiot," Patsy sniffed, with a dismissive scowl at Indhira. "You oughtn't to let her touch any of your nice things—she'll only spoil them."

Did I detect a note of jealousy in Patsy's voice? Of course I did. Foolish Patsy has always fondly imagined herself to belong to me more completely than any of my sluts, and by some twisted logic has assumed a kind of imaginary ownership of me. Her possessiveness and jealousy sometimes assume quite amusing levels of violence, and it was not difficult to see that Patsy was actually engineering Indhira's clumsiness so that the Indian girl would lose favor with me.

As Indhira bent to pick up the next box, Patsy gave

her a shove which sent her sprawling, almost knocking over one of the bell jars in which were growing a collection of fragile, precious plants.

"Clumsy little bitch!" Patsy smirked.

This time, the meek Indhira sprang to her feet with a cry of outrage.

"You are ill-bred and hateful!" she exclaimed.

"Hark who's talking!" Patsy sneered. "The little gutter-snipe who used to sleep with the cows!"

Indhira could stand no more and, striking out at Patsy, she seized a great handful of her hair. Patsy countered with a kick to Indhira's shins and, as the Indian girl stumbled sideways, she ripped a great long tear down the back of her embroidered sari blouse, baring the freshly tattooed "CD" of Indhira's proud submission.

I chose this moment to intervene. Diverting though it might be to watch two half-naked girls fighting like tiger-cubs, I could not risk any damage to my possessions, which were to prove far more precious than either of the brainless sluts were capable of imagining.

"You will desist in this foolish bickering!" I said coldly, stepping between the two girls. "Immediately."

I looked from Patsy to Indhira and back again. Indhira was already trembling under my gaze, whilst Patsy's bravado was visibly wilting in the sudden realization of her own foolishness.

"Mistress," Indhira whimpered, a curl of Patsy's mud-brown hair hanging from her guilty fingers.

"It was her fault," cut in Patsy. "Stupid little bitch. You should've left her in the sewer with the rats."

"Silence!" My leather-gloved hand swept across Patsy's face, knocking the breath from her and leaving a reddening imprint on her cheek. "You are two stupid and impudent sluts, and I shall have to discipline you." I smiled. "Both of you."

"B-But Mistress…" Indhira ventured, her face tragic with injustice.

"Both of you," I repeated. "Severely."

I walked around the two girls, surveying the damage they had wrought.

"Fortunately, nothing is broken," I conceded. "But that is no thanks to you. Bend over the trunk."

The two sluts exchanged glances. Indhira obeyed me instantly, but Patsy defied me with a sullen stare.

"Must I force you to obey me?"

Reluctantly, Patsy bent forward over the side of the trunk.

"Lift up your skirts. Quickly now!"

As Patsy raised her skirts, it was clear why she had been so slow to obey me. Whereas Indhira was naked underneath her sari, her only adornment the tattoos and piercings of her ownership, Patsy's ample bumcheeks were covered by a pair of crumpled linen drawers, sewn closed at the crotch and covering her almost to the knees.

"So," I said quietly. "You have seen fit to disobey me yet again."

Patsy wriggled uncomfortably as I selected one of my favourite malacca canes and used its tip to trace the contours of her sex.

"Ma'am...don't!" she protested as I dug it rather hard into her flesh at a precise spot between her buttocks, knowing how she hated the pleasure it gave her to be touched there.

"I shall do exactly as I please," I replied. "And since you are my possession, you will behave exactly as I instruct you to behave. Is that perfectly clear?"

A second jab of the cane was enough to secure a moan of assent from Patsy.

"'Twas only that I didn't want other women seeing my...you know...seeing me there," she protested.

"Hold your tongue, lest you condemn yourself still further."

I contemplated the two backsides presented so beautifully for chastisement. Each was alluring and stimulating in its own way: Indhira's small, rounded cheeks with their skin of caramel-gold, so firm and springy; Patsy's coarser, ampler charms, with their dimpled flesh rippling so invitingly underneath the false modesty of her drawers. Such pleasure could be derived so simply. Ah, but where to begin? That was the tantalizing, intoxicating question.

The tip of the cane was razor-sharp, and the cotton of Patsy's drawers thin and of poor quality. It tore easily at a skillful jab of the cane, rending from waist to crotch with a soft whispering sound.

Underneath, Patsy's nethercheeks were creamy-white and quivering with anticipation. Her thighs were slightly parted, and I could see from the damp cotton between them that she was moist with expectation.

"Your arsecheeks are perfectly white," I commented dispassionately, running the tip of the cane over them in exploratory maneuvers. "Evidently it is far too long since I last beat you."

Patsy's body tensed, no doubt expecting that she was to receive the first, blessed blow from the cane. Which is precisely why I turned my attentions to the hapless Indhira, who throughout all this time had been standing perfectly still and silent, awaiting her fate.

"And what have you to say for yourself, slut?" I demanded, stroking the cane very slowly down Indhira's back until it rested in the deep crevice between her buttocks.

"I—I am very sorry, Mistress."

"And what else?" I exerted a little more pressure with the tip of the cane, and it slipped a fraction of an inch into the tiny, tight hole of her anus. I felt Indhira tremble beneath my touch.

"F-Forgive me, Mistress."

"Perhaps I shall. Perhaps not." I began twisting the cane, knowing how it must torment her to feel it winding round and round just inside her forbidden gate, possessing and yet not satisfying. "You are a clumsy slut, Indhira."

"Yes, Mistress."

"A clumsy, careless, insolent slut. Say it."

"I am a clumsy, careless, insolent slut. Mistress. Oh, Mistress, please forgive me."

But I was tired of Indhira's pathetic protestations. Sensing how much she longed for me to beat her and bugger her, possess her, and so satisfy her desperate desire for complete degradation, I removed the cane from her arse and stood back.

"Mistress?" Indhira raised her head and looked at me over her shoulders. Her eyes were full of longing. Beside her, I could hear Patsy's breathing, hoarse and shallow; awaiting the ecstasy of the first, blissful cane-stroke across her bare backside. "Are you going to beat us now?"

A slow smile crept to my lips. A smile of delicious, insatiable cruelty.

"No," I replied. "No, I don't think I shall. I think I shall simply leave you here for a few hours, to ponder the consequences of disobedience."

"But, Mistress!"

"And mark my words well. If either of you should move one inch from this spot, your punishment will not be a beating; it will be banishment from my service."

From the journal of Elizabeth Stanbridge:
The following morning, a little before dawn, I awoke in

my rooms to discover Phoebe Milnrow curled up beside me in my bed.

It took a moment for the truth to filter into my consciousness. How could I have done such a thing—taking advantage of this innocent girl in the heat of my anger against Annabella Fitzgerald? Remorse flooded my soul as I remembered the violence of my passion. I had done precisely what I had sworn to myself I would not do, and I was not proud of my actions.

But, as I told myself, it was not too late to make amends. I was not and never would be Claudia Dungarrow. And so it was that when Phoebe awoke, I proceeded to make love to her with the utmost gentleness.

"Ah, ah, Miss Elizabeth," she sighed, her face filled with wonderment as I knelt between her legs and began lapping like a kitten at her sex. "That feels…oh! Oh, it feels so wonderful—whatever are you doing to me?"

"I am gamahuching you," I smiled, and kissed her again between the lips of her sex. They were perhaps a little pink and swollen, but showed little sign of the violence with which I had deflowered her. "I am not hurting you?"

"Oh, no, not at all!"

"You must tell me if I am doing you any harm."

"Oh, Miss Elizabeth, it doesn't hurt in the least. It feels…it feels just heavenly."

She came in a torrent of soft oohs and aahs, snuggled

into the crook of my arms and fell asleep. When she awoke again, an hour later, it was dangerously close to the time when the servants would rise and be about their duties.

"You must go back to your own room," I told her, helping her into one of my nightdresses—her own being too creased and soiled to be presentable.

"But why can't I stay here with you?"

"Because…Because it is far too dangerous!"

"I don't understand!"

"Hush, Phoebe, and do as I say. What we have done…there are those who would not approve, you must not speak of it. Now, hurry—before someone finds you here."

I succeeded in persuading Phoebe that she must go back to her own room, and had almost convinced myself that all danger was past, when who should happen along but old Mrs. Wilkins, the housekeeper, just at the very moment when Phoebe was emerging from my room. She greeted the sight with a look of great curiosity.

"Whatever are you doing there, Miss Phoebe?"

Phoebe opened her mouth to chirp a reply, but I succeeded in getting in first.

"Poor dear Phoebe had a terrible nightmare last night. She came to me for comfort, didn't you, Phoebe?"

To my relief, Phoebe nodded. "Miss Elizabeth has been so kind to me."

"Poor child," tut-tutted Mrs. Wilkins, taking Phoebe

by the arm. "Yes, to be sure, she does look rather pale. I'll have the doctor make up a dose for her. She'll be right as rain by teatime."

It is almost a month since I seduced Phoebe Milnrow, and almost exactly the same length of time since I saw or had any communication with my dear Demelza.

Phoebe is attentive and loving; and I confess that I have—from time to time—continued her lessons in sensual education. She is an apt and willing pupil and, for my part, I feel a responsibility to right the wrong I did her in relieving her of her virginity.

But this afternoon, during our piano lesson, I received a most disturbing communication: one which put poor Phoebe entirely out of my mind.

A knock came on the door about three o'clock, and I signaled to Phoebe to halt her practice.

"Come in."

The door opened, and Mrs. Wilkins's round red face appeared in the doorway.

"There's a letter for you," she announced, handing it to me. "Came by hand, it did." Curiosity was written all over her face. "'Must be something important,' I said to myself. 'I'll take it to Miss Stanbridge myself.'"

"Thank you," I said absentmindedly, as the door closed behind Mrs. Wilkins. I walked across to the French windows and tore open the envelope. Phoebe skipped up beside me.

"What is it? Who is it from?"

"Please, Phoebe. Continue your practice."

"But…" Phoebe protested rather peevishly.

"Now! Please."

I read the letter a second time, not quite able to absorb its full implications. And yet the wording was simple enough:

HOW LONG IS IT SINCE YOU SAW DEMELZA, ELIZABETH? I WONDER HOW SHE IS. C.

C. C for Claudia…

Horror overwhelmed me, my heart thumping in my chest. Why was Claudia Dungarrow writing to me now, after all these long months of silence and freedom? And what could she possibly mean by the cryptic wording of her letter?

Of one thing alone I was certain. I must seek out Demelza and reassure myself that she was all right. For, in my heart of hearts, I was certain that something terrible must have happened to her.

CHAPTER 4

From the journal of Elizabeth Stanbridge:

Days passed. I yearned to get away, to seek out Demelza and satisfy myself that she was unharmed, but duty kept me at Milnrow House. My next half-day's leave would not fall due until the coming Saturday, so I had three more days of agony to wait.

The words of Claudia's note burned in my mind and would not let me be still. Had it been some cruel hoax, subtly designed to trouble my every waking and sleeping thought, or had Claudia indeed done some terrible harm to my beloved Demelza?

I sent a telegram to Demelza, but received no reply. My agitation grew more apparent daily. Even poor

Phoebe suffered from my burgeoning anxiety, hurt and bemused by my indifference to her girlish concern.

"Miss Elizabeth," she coaxed, edging closer to me as I tried in vain to concentrate on the theme I was marking.

"What is it now?" I demanded peevishly. "Have you not work enough to be getting on with?"

"Y-Yes, Mademoiselle Elizabeth. But—"

"But what?"

"I am worried about you. You have grown so thin and pale, are you ill?"

"I am quite well, thank you."

"Then you are angry with me?"

"No, Phoebe, I am not angry with you. But I may become angry if you do not attend to your studies!"

"Oh, why do you turn me away?" Phoebe's brown eyes were softly misted with tears. "What has upset you so?"

I heaved a sigh, half of annoyance and half of remorse. I knew full well that I was treating Phoebe abominably. What crime had the poor child committed, save that of diverting my thoughts from Demelza Fitzgerald?

"All is well," I told her, patting her hand as kindly as I could manage. "You need not concern yourself about me; I am quite capable of taking care of myself."

Phoebe went back to her desk with evident reluctance, half-turning back toward me as if about to say something, then thinking better of it and returning to her books.

I thought the episode past and forgotten—until this

afternoon, when I received a summons from Phoebe's mother, Lady Jocasta Fallowfield.

"Mistress wants to see you," announced Mrs. Wilkins; and I thought I detected a hint of smug satisfaction in her tone.

"But—why?"

"Mistress doesn't confide in me, miss, I'm sure," replied the housekeeper. "I'd have thought you'd know, you being so friendly with her daughter and all."

I felt my cheeks redden at this sly jibe, but turned my head away and finished packing away my papers.

"I'll be there directly," I told her.

"Well, you'd best look sharp," Mrs. Wilkins replied in her parting shot. "She's not in the mood for being kept waiting."

It was with some trepidation that I knocked on the parlor door a few moments later.

"Come in."

I entered the room. Lady Fallowfield was standing by the window, a fine, imposing figure in her early forties, a little above average height and very straight and slender in her mauve and black silk day dress. She turned slowly toward me at my approach, her face expressionless.

"Ah. Stanbridge."

I inclined my head respectfully. "You wished to see me, Lady Fallowfield?"

"Indeed." She cleared her throat with a ladylike cough.

53

"Pray close the door behind you. I would not wish what I have to say to be overheard by the servants."

"As you wish, madam." My heart raced, but I tried hard to conceal my apprehension.

"My daughter has revealed certain facts to me," Jocasta Fallowfield began. "Certain intimate facts regarding your relationship with her."

Suddenly my mouth became dry. Panic rose in my throat, contracting it so tightly that I found myself quite unable to speak.

"She tells me," continued my employer, "that you have relieved her of her virginity and instructed her in certain...intimate practices...which may be practiced by one woman upon another. Is this true?"

Lady Fallowfield's eyes bored into me. I quaked, but forced myself to hold my head up.

"Yes, madam," I whispered. "It is entirely true."

"She tells me also that you have exercised the most rigorous discipline upon her person. Is this correct?"

"I fear it is, madam."

I fully expected Lady Fallowfield to explode into a torrent of righteous anger—after all, her temper is quite legendary—but, to my amazement, she smiled coolly.

"Excellent. At last my prayers are answered."

"I beg your pardon?"

"I was beginning to wonder, Stanbridge, if my daughter was possessed of natural affections toward the female sex. It was, in fact, my concern for her sensual welfare which prompted me to engage you as her governess."

"Madam? I do not understand."

"You are a very attractive and sensual young woman.
Were I ten years younger, I myself—but that matters not.
The fact is that I engaged you in the hope that you
would have a proper understanding of your duties and
give her the very broadest education, as my own
governess gave to me."

"I...see. You are pleased that I have initiated Elizabeth into the Sapphic arts?"

"Indeed, I am most indebted to you, Miss Stanbridge.
However..." Lady Fallowfield's tone changed from one
of warm congratulation to one of regret.

"There is a problem, your Ladyship?"

"I fear so, Stanbridge. You see, my daughter is a rather
silly young girl, quite naïve and oversensitive. She has
become uncommonly attached to you. As a result, the
punishments and disciplines you have lavished upon
her have caused her to become extremely...distressed.

"Should she confide her distress to others... I am
sure you will appreciate, Miss Stanbridge, that the
potential for scandal is enormous. And with my position
in society at stake... I cannot afford to take risks, no
matter how attached I may be to certain members of my
household."

I began to understand what Lady Fallowfield was
conveying to me, in the most circumspect of terms.

"Am I to be dismissed, madam?"

Lady Fallowfield sighed.

"You cannot imagine with what regret I am forced to do this, Elizabeth. Let us simply agree that you have decided to resign—a family illness, perhaps, or an unfulfilled desire to travel. I will give you six months' salary and the most favorable reference any governess could possibly desire. You will not have any difficulty in obtaining another position."

In all honesty, my employer's words caused me more relief than distress. I had feared that I was about to be ejected in disgrace from Milnrow House, yet now I was being offered a small measure of financial independence which would allow me to leave immediately and seek Demelza.

"Thank you, your Ladyship." I curtsied low. "I will of course work out my notice."

"There will be no need for that, Elizabeth." She took my hand and carried it briefly to her lips. "You may leave whenever you wish." She smiled. "Ah, Elizabeth. If only circumstances were a little less…constrained."

I left the drawing room with my head in a whirl. On my way up the stairs to my rooms, I almost collided with Phoebe, her hair disheveled and her eyes pink from weeping.

"Oh, Miss Elizabeth," she sniffled. "Has Mamma been very cruel to you? She has not driven you away?"

"I shall be leaving this evening," I replied brusquely. Phoebe's face fell even further.

"No!" she cried. "Oh, it is all my fault! I knew I should not have spoken to Mamma, but I was upset when you did not return my affections."

I took Phoebe's small, white hand in mine. It was a child's hand, as immature and tender as its owner.

"You will soon find another lover," I promised her with gentle reassurance. "Many lovers." And, drawing her close to me, I lavished upon her lips the most passionate and lingering of farewell kisses.

Upon leaving Milnrow House, I hired a carriage and went directly to Lady Annabella Fitzgerald's home. It was very late when I arrived, but one light still burned in an upstairs window.

As I stood upon the steps of the Hall, I asked myself what foolishness had brought me here. What reason did I have to suspect that Demelza was in any danger at all, other than the cryptic note I had received from Claudia— if indeed it was from Claudia at all, and not just some silly practical joke?

After ringing the bell many times and waiting for what seemed an eternity, I heard the sound of footsteps coming toward the door, along the tiled hallway. A key turned slowly in the lock; then the door swung inward. I was astonished to find myself confronted not by Annabella's housemaid, but by Annabella herself, in her nightdress and with her long blonde hair hanging over her shoulder in a waist-long braid.

"You took your time in coming," she said dryly, unable to keep the hostility from her voice. But there was more than hostility in her tone, and her expression betrayed fear and anxiety.

"You were expecting me?" I stepped into the hallway and Annabella closed the door behind me.

"From the moment I received a letter from Claudia Dungarrow."

I gasped.

"You...she wrote to you? About Demelza?"

"Follow me."

Without another word, Annabella led the way up the stairs, her lantern casting eerie patterns on the walls. I could almost imagine the laughing face of Claudia Dungarrow, mocking me from among the dancing shadows.

"Demelza is in here."

For a moment, my heart leapt. If Demelza was still safe at home with her sister, surely no serious harm could have befallen her. But my joy turned to horror as I stepped into the bedroom.

Demelza was lying very still and white in the old four-poster bed, candlelight illuminating her face. At first I thought she was sleeping, but as I stepped closer I saw that her eyes were wide open and staring, her mouth curved into a secret smile, as though she could see something wonderful beyond the shadows which surrounded the bed.

"Demelza!" I rushed to her bedside. I touched her hand as it lay across the coverlet, but she did not move.

"She cannot hear you," Annabella said quietly.

"But how…why…? What has happened to her?"

Annabella sank down onto the bed, taking her sister's hand.

"Five days ago, a huge bouquet of damask roses was delivered to the house. The card read: 'To my darling Demelza, with all my love.' The moment she breathed in the scent, she swooned away, and no one has been able to rouse her." I saw Annabella's lips tremble. "And then, three days ago, I received this note."

Even before I read it, I knew that it was from Claudia Dungarrow; I would have recognized that arrogant, swirling hand anywhere. With terrible apprehension, I unfolded the single sheet of white paper.

IS DEAR DEMELZA UNWELL? OH, POOR DARLING SLUT. SHE HAS ONE MONTH—NO LONGER. CATCH ME IF YOU CAN. C.

"Claudia!" I hissed, screwing up the paper and hurling it away from me in horror and disgust. "The evil hellcat…"

Our eyes met. Without even speaking, we knew that fate was forcing us into an unwilling alliance, and that for Demelza's sake, we would have to bury our differences and strive together.

But it would not be easy to overcome our jealousy and our mistrust. Only our love of Demelza and our mutual hatred of Claudia Dungarrow could prevent us from destroying each other even before our quest had begun.

From the journal of Claudia Dungarrow:
Ah, night. Sweet, soft, dark, and mysterious. Darkness is my natural element. In it I move swiftly and easily, unseen and unsuspected.

The summer night was hot and heavy, the air sticky with flower scents and filled with the lazy drone of insects. No one saw me as I crossed the lawn, a shadow within a shadow, a silent predator in search of the most delicious prey.

It was simplicity itself to gain entrance to Annabella Fitzgerald's house. The fools were sleeping as I climbed the stairs to Demelza's room, pushing the door open softly and slipping inside.

Naturally, they had not thought to guard her. She lay quite alone, the guttering candles beside the bed casting pallid shadows on her perfectly beautiful face. How radiantly she smiled! For the darling slut was dreaming of me....

"Darling slut, pretty darling slut, you are entirely mine. Mine forever." I stroked her face, savoring the cool smoothness of her skin, cool as stone. Cool as death. And I sighed with the delicious pleasure of knowing her mine absolutely and eternally.

60

I worked swiftly, opening my bag and taking out a long dark-brown seedpod. Holding it between my fingers, I raised it over Demelza's face and began to crush it. It crackled softly and began to fragment, releasing a golden-yellow elixir which seeped out and trickled down over my fingers.

"Sweet slut. Pretty little pet. Wake for your Mistress…"

One drop of the oily liquor was all it took; one drop, placed upon Demelza's lips. A few seconds later, she drew in a long, deep, luxurious breath, sighed, and parted her lips, her tongue flicking out to lick up the potent oil.

Its effect was striking. The glazed, faraway look departed from her eyes, and she leapt up from the bed, clawing and gasping as she sought desperately to lick the rest of the liquid from my fingers.

"Not so fast, my pretty one," I laughed. And, drawing away, I unbuttoned my cloak and let it slither to the floor.

Underneath, I was naked save for patent-leather boots, very high in the heel and pointed in the toe; molded close to the calf with scarlet laces. The sultry night air caressed my skin, and I took a moment to revel in my own nakedness, the sheer joy of my infinite sensual power.

Demelza was writhing on the bed, moaning now, her lips parted in a kind of childlike keening. She formed no recognizable words, but I knew the source of her

61

distress, the need which only her Mistress could satisfy.

"In a moment dear slut." I smiled. "In a moment you shall have what you crave, and more."

The oil glistened wetly on the palms of my hands. Slowly and languorously, I smeared it between my breasts and down my belly, ending at the dark triangle between my thighs. And then I knelt upon the bed, lowering myself onto Demelza's writhing body.

"Ah. Ah, yes, yes, yes!" she sighed and murmured, her tongue lapping greedily, insatiably, at the oil smeared over my skin.

"Drink deep, little one. Let desire possess your soul."

The pleasure, I confess, was intense. Demelza's tongue was skillful and tireless, enraptured and enslaved by the potent Eastern oil. Its muscular tip lapped and teased its way from the valley of my breasts to the small, deep well of my navel, sending shivers of gratification through my body. I am no stranger to pleasure, for I have tasted every dark perversion, every secret fetish, every forbidden ecstasy; yet this simple piquant amusement afforded me the most intense satisfaction.

Slowly, flesh slithered over flesh. Demelza's tongue wound its way down my belly to the mossy mound of my pubis.

"Good slut, obedient slut," I purred, sliding my hands beneath Demelza's head and pushing it hard against my sex.

I had no need to force her. She was whimpering with

the desire to enter me with her tongue, and I had not the heart to refuse her this small indulgence. Indeed, I assisted her in her duty by easing apart the petals of my womanhood and urging her to lap at my nectar. This she did with the prettiest sighs and moans, wriggling and darting her tongue into the deepest heart of me.

My self-control is such that I succeeded in holding myself on the very brink of ecstasy for many long minutes before at last allowing the teasing of Demelza's lips and tongue to bring me to complete gratification. The dear little slut was weeping with gratitude as I laid her down on the bed gently and covered her with the sheet.

"You see how kind your Mistress is to her faithful sluts," I whispered. And Demelza smiled and sighed, as though, even in her trance, she understood.

"Mistress...my Mistress..." she mouthed silently.

"You will sleep now."

Taking a pouch of white powder from my bag, I measured a teaspoonful into the palm of my hand and blew it into Demelza's face like a fragrant kiss.

She sighed and sank bank onto her pillows, falling back into a radiant, unseeing ecstasy. With a final kiss upon her sleeping brow, I fastened on my cloak and departed, melting into the night from whence I had come.

CHAPTER 5

From the journal of Elizabeth Stanbridge:
"We may be forced to work together for my poor sister's sake," declared Annabella. "But I shall not spend one more second in your company than is absolutely necessary."

And so Annabella and I have decided to begin our investigations separately. Singly, we shall cover more ground than we could together; besides, I have no greater fondness for Annabella than she harbors for me.

It seemed natural to begin by returning to the very source of all my woes: the house to which Claudia Dungarrow had taken me after my abduction, there to train me in all the arts of submission and sensual depravity.

The Manor stands a few miles outside the university

city of Cambridge, beside the river at Grantchester. As I
stepped down from my carriage, a shiver of recognition
ran over my flesh. Although I knew that the Manor was
no longer in Claudia's possession, her very essence
seemed to pervade every stone, wafting in coils about
me, like a sweet, evil incense.

I scolded myself for trembling as I climbed the steps
to the front door. After all, what could there possibly be
to fear in this place? It was a house, nothing more; and
houses cannot tell tales of innocence depraved, or stolen
maidenheads.

The bellpull summoned up a faraway tolling sound
which seemed to echo through the house. Perhaps it
was empty; perhaps no one was living here—it certainly
seemed very quiet and deserted. After ringing a second
time, I hesitated, almost convincing myself that I had
done my duty in coming here and could now leave with
all honor intact. But my relief was short-lived. Soft footsteps sounded on the tiles of the hallway. I caught my
breath as the latch clicked open.

"Good day to you, madam."

I blinked. The face which greeted me was neither
that of Claudia, nor Patsy her maid, nor of any English
housemaid I had ever encountered. It was caramel-
skinned, a fragile oval dominated by a pair of the
hugest, most radiant dark eyes imaginable. Only an
effort of will freed me from the glorious captivity of
those eyes, so innocently sensual.

"Good day. I...have come to see your mistress."

"The master and mistress are away."

"And when will they return?"

"I do not know, madam. The mistress has left me in charge of the house."

"I see." I contemplated the Indian girl with more interest than one might normally take in a housemaid. She was, undeniably, one of the loveliest young women I had set eyes on in a very long time; and her loveliness transcended the merely physical. The look in her eyes hinted at unusual sensual depths. "And who might you be?"

The lowered eyes looked up at me through a long sweep of black lashes.

"My name is Indhira, madam."

I thought quickly, guessing that Indhira was a girl who craved approval and would not wish to anger me.

"I am...considering purchasing the Manor," I lied, hoping that I sounded convincing.

"Purchasing the house, madam? But—"

"And I had hoped to inspect the house this morning. But since your master and mistress are not here..."

I paused. Indhira smiled at me, nervous as a gazelle but as eager to please as I could have hoped.

"I could show you the house, madam. If you wish..."

"Splendid." I patted her hand and stepped into the hallway, suppressing a rising shudder of panic as I breathed in the old, remembered scents of fresh flowers, beeswax polish and fine leather. "You are a very good girl, Indhira. I shall speak favorably of your behaviour to your mistress."

A faint blush of gratification appeared on Indhira's dusky complexion, and I instantly regretted my white lie.

"Shall we begin, madam?"

"Of course. I have a particular interest in the first-floor rooms. The old schoolroom, for example…"

Indhira led the way through rooms I remembered only too well. The drawing room with its French doors, leading out onto a sunny terrace. The music room. The stairwell, once lined with engravings and ink sketches of daring obscenity—now replaced by tedious oil paintings of kittens in baskets.

"I…was slightly acquainted with the previous owner of the Manor," mentioned casually as we climbed the stairs to the schoolroom. My heart thumped traitorously in my chest, refusing to play along with my charade of seeming calm.

"Indeed, madam?"

"Indeed. I believe she was a learned lady, a doctor of physical sciences at Cambridge University. Have you any idea what became of her after she sold the Manor?"

I searched the dusky face but there was no flicker of understanding.

"No, madam. I was brought here from Jaipur by my master and mistress. I know little of the Manor before then." She paused at the door of the schoolroom. "You wish to see inside, madam? The door is locked, but I have a key."

"Certainly."

My pulse raced as I visualized the scene on the other side of the door. The schoolroom which Claudia had created for the express purpose of taming and instructing me; and the room beyond, more terrible and more exciting still. And the punishment room, my ingenious and luxurious prison for so many long days, until at last my spirit yielded and I submitted to Claudia's inexorable will....

But surely these rooms would have changed almost beyond recognition. Surely no one in possession of their senses would preserve them in their original state?

I gasped as I stepped into the schoolroom. It was complete in every detail, exactly as I remembered it; as though Claudia had only just completed one of her "lessons" and dismissed her pupils for the rest of the day.

A row of wooden school desks and benches ran across the room, facing the teacher's desk, taller than the rest and raised up on a low dais. On the wall behind hung a fine array of instruments of chastisement, carefully selected by Claudia for their efficacy in disciplining errant young girls.

I stepped forward and stretched out a hand, stroking a supple cane lightly. The scents of linseed oil and sex floated in the sun-warmed air, and I breathed in deeply, carried away on a wave of nostalgia, feeling once again the hungry bite of the cane on my flesh. I had almost forgotten Indhira until she spoke.

"You have been here before, madam?"

I half-turned to look at her. Her eyes were round and full of curiosity, devouring the strange and wonderful things she could see hanging on the walls all around her. Paddles and straps; whips and canes; manacles and exquisitely made chastity harnesses in jeweled silver.

"Oh yes, Indhira. Many times."

"These things...they are...so—"

"What, Indhira?"

"So beautiful."

"You have never seen them before?"

"Hardly ever, madam. Usually I am not allowed to enter the schoolroom, I only have the key because there is no one else to take care of the house."

"This room is exactly as I remember it from my last visit. Why were these things not taken away when your master and mistress bought the Manor?"

"I do not know, madam. But I heard only last week that they had been sold."

"Sold!" I gazed around the room. Strange purchases indeed; I burned to know about the purchaser.

"Yes, madam. To a lady."

"Her name, Indhira."

"I...Merriman, that was it, madam. Eone Merriman."

"Tell me of this lady. Where does she live? Where can I find her?"

"That is all I know of her, madam. Only her name."

Disappointed, I turned away. Still, even a name was better than nothing, and I sensed that I must find this mysterious Eone Merriman if I wished to know more about Claudia Dungarrow. Perhaps the schoolroom itself would yield more clues.

And so I began my search, each rediscovered item awaking memories of pleasure and pain. The silken cords with which Claudia had so often bound me to a chair or a sawhorse; the dog collar and leash with which she had humiliated me when I had been particularly recalcitrant; the soft white leather gloves, one palm covered with velvet, the other with sharpened metal spikes.

"What are you doing, madam? Will you permit me to help you?" Her voice was a sultry, appreciative sigh as I opened Claudia's punishment cabinet and began rediscovering what lay within. "W-What are those, madam?" she inquired, coming up close beside me and gazing wonderingly at the ingenious array of toys.

"These, Indhira?" I held out my hand so that she could see more clearly. "You have not seen these before?"

"No, madam."

"These are clamps, my dear. Tit-clamps. They are fastened on the nipples as a…discipline."

"Oh. Oh, madam…" I could see the lust deepening in her eyes, felt her quickening breath on my cheek, and knew that Indhira was a true-born submissive, truly happy only when offering up her body and her soul to her Mistress's will. "And how do they feel? Is the pain very great?"

"Would you like to try them on your own titties?"

"Oh, Madam…could I? Dare I…?"

"Of course. Lift up your sari blouse and bare your breasts."

She did so with shaking hands, her lips moist with excitement, her breath shallow and rapid.

"Like this, Madam?"

"Precisely. Now take a deep breath, and try not to cry out."

I opened up the clamps and let them spring shut on Indhira's brownish-pink nipples. Such nipples they were: long and tough as betel nuts, placed jauntily on wide-set, uptilted breasts that were rather full on such a slender frame.

The dear girl did not squeal or shout as the rough-toothed clamps snapped shut on her flesh. She had either been well trained, or had an innate love of pain (I suspect both). Indhira let out only a long, shuddering sigh that seemed to speak both of agony and ecstasy, and as her eyelids closed I saw the bright beads of tears sparkling on her lashes.

"Oh, madam," she murmured as her eyes slowly opened. "Oh, madam, the feelings…I cannot describe them!"

She swayed slightly, and I slipped my arm about her waist to steady her.

"It is too much for you to bear?" I asked her, concerned that she might be unused to such an intensity of sensations.

"Oh no, madam! I would bear so much more, if only—"

"If only, Indhira?"

"If only you would show me how."

"Dear girl. Dear, sweet child."

I smiled at her and kissed her gently on the brow. How could I refuse such a charming appeal?

From the journal of Claudia Dungarrow:

I confess that it amused me greatly to watch the little pantomime enacted between my once-dear slut, Elizabeth, and the servant girl, Indhira. It pleased and satisfied me to see Elizabeth so eager to follow in her teacher's footsteps, practicing her hard-won skills so ably on the eager body of my Indian serving wench.

But that was a mere amusement. How much more it gratified me to follow that haughty bitch, Annabella Fitzgerald, to my old Cambridge college and watch, unseen, as she attempted to pick up my trail.

I had primed the trap with delicious bait. Annabella's inquiries at St. Matilda's College led her to my former colleague and intimate friend, Dr. Tanith Beresford, who greeted her with somewhat less than sisterly warmth.

Annabella knocked upon the door of Tanith's rooms, and waited. Eventually the door opened, and my dear friend appeared at her door, very statuesque and dramatic in a close-fitting gown of midnight-blue velvet, overlaid with a tippet of silver fox.

"Well, well. Lady Annabella Fitzgerald," she remarked coldly, her eyes as pale and green as glaciers.

"Dr. Beresford? I am looking for Claudia Dungarrow."

A faint sneer animated Tanith Beresford's aristocratic and handsome features.

"Then you can hardly expect to find her here."

"But you...I was led to believe that you and she—"

The sneer turned to a mocking laughter.

"Are you implying some scandalous connection? I hardly think you are in any position to claim moral superiority, Lady Annabella. You, who were drummed out of this college for committing the most disgraceful improprieties with its students!"

At this reminder of her own degeneracy, Annabella colored—and I had to stifle my own laughter, lest I gave myself away. Now that the game was afoot, and all the pieces set out so prettily, it would never do to upset the board.

"May I come in?"

Tanith did not reply, but turned and walked back into her rooms, leaving Annabella to follow in her wake. Paying not the slightest attention to Annabella, Tanith proceeded to pour herself a glass of dry sherry.

"Dr. Beresford...about Claudia."

Tanith glanced up.

"You are beginning to irritate me with your constant whining, Annabella."

Anger flashed in Annabella's steel-grey eyes, but she bit her lip and forced herself to be polite.

"My sister is very ill, Dr. Beresford. Dangerously so. She may even be near death. I have good reason to believe that Claudia Dungarrow is the cause of it."

"And why should this tale of woe be of any interest to me?"

"You are a friend of Claudia's."

"So you seem determined to insist."

"Have you no honor and no shame?" exclaimed Annabella, dashing the sherry glass from Tanith Beresford's hand. "Do you care nothing for an innocent girl and her sister, brought to despair by that evil bitch, Claudia?"

Tanith's eyes narrowed to slits. Pleasure and desire coursed through my veins. It is when she is at her most malevolent that Tanith Beresford is also at her most alluring.

"Take care how you speak of my friends, if you care anything for your precious sister," she hissed.

There was a spark of hope in Annabella's eyes.

"You know where Claudia is—you do!"

"Perhaps." The sneer turned to a satisfied smile. There can be few pleasures greater than wielding complete power over another human being. "Perhaps not."

"Tell me where she is."

"Why should I?"

"Because…because of Demelza, my poor sister…"

"Get down on your knees. Beg me to tell you."

"No!"

"Then leave now. And close the door behind you, I do so hate sitting in a draught."

A vein, pulsing at Annabella's temple, was the only outward sign of her inner turmoil as she sank to her knees before Tanith Beresford.

"Please tell me where Claudia is."

"I told you to beg. Do it, Annabella. Beg me for your sister's worthless life."

"Please, Dr. Beresford. Please help me; there is no one else."

"You are a worthless slut, Annabella. Say it."

"I…I am a…worthless slut."

"Louder, I can scarcely hear you."

"A worthless slut."

"And you are not worthy to lick my arse. Your Mistress's arse. Say it."

"N-Not worthy…"

"Say it!"

Annabella raised her head. There was genuine hatred in her steely eyes.

"I am not worthy to lick your arse. Mistress."

"Good. At last we understand each other." Tanith went over to the table and poured herself another glass of sherry. "You are a handsome enough slut, Annabella, but you have somewhat too high an opinion of yourself. Small wonder Claudia cast you aside."

"She did nothing of the kind!"

Tanith's hand struck Annabella a glancing blow across the cheek, just hard enough to shock her into silence and leave the reddening print of five vengeful fingers.

"Hold your tongue, Annabella. Don't you want me to tell you where Claudia is?"

The deceiving ray of hope lit up Annabella's face once more.

"Yes. Oh, yes!"

"Yes, *Mistress.*"

"Please, Mistress. Tell me, Mistress."

Tanith Beresford looked at the kneeling figure of Annabella and kicked out at her, landing her booted foot square in the middle of her chest and sending her sprawling. She laughed heartily to see Annabella's complete discomfiture.

"I cannot," she said.

"You…?"

"I have not the faintest idea where Claudia is."

Annabella's eyes blazed with fury.

"And all this time you…?"

Tanith raised her hand for silence.

"I do not know, but I know someone who does." She sipped at her dry sherry, making the moment last. "Her name is Eone Merriman."

From the journal of Elizabeth Stanbridge:
From unpromising beginnings, Annabella and I have culled the seeds of success.

The following day, we met, as agreed, to discuss our next move. At once it became clear that we must begin by tracing the elusive Eone Merriman.

Not quite as elusive as we might have imagined, for it quickly transpired that Eone Merriman was the principal dancer with the Sadler's Wells Royal Ballet. And so we travelled together down to London—for neither of us trusted the other sufficiently to risk allowing her to meet the woman alone.

After the performance of *Swan Lake*, Annabella and I arranged to be taken backstage to meet the prima ballerina. Her dresser ushered us into her dressing room.

"Mademoiselle Merriman is attending to her toilette."

"Then perhaps we should wait until she is ready to receive us?"

The dresser shook her head.

"Not at all, madam. She is always at her most…sociable following a successful performance."

We were somewhat surprised to discover Eone Merriman reclining in a large zinc hip-bath in the middle of the dressing-room floor, her body very pink and appetizing amid a sea of creamy bubbles. She shook out her corn-blonde locks and stretched out one long limb, pointing her toe as she ran the cake of soap up and down it.

"Ah—my public!" she giggled, pouting coquettishly.

"You were wonderful tonight!" I assured her, without the slightest shadow of a lie. Eone Merriman was undoubtedly a very fine dancer.

"It was an excellent performance," Annabella agreed. "But that is not the only reason why we have come to see you."

"Oh, really?" Eone pulled a face like a disappointed child's. She was indeed very childlike—fragile, capricious, captivating.

"We are trying to find out the whereabouts of an…old friend," I hazarded. "Her name is Claudia Dungarrow—you know her, I believe?"

"Now let me see." The cake of soap travelled along one slender, perfect arm and circled a small, apple-hard breast, stiff-stalked and very kissable. "Yes, I believe I may have heard the name."

The little tease was playing with us—that much was plain. But I knew that we must not push too hard, for fear that she would simply refuse to help us. Besides, it was difficult to dislike her. There was a freshness and mischievousness about her which I could not help finding rather alluring.

"We really do need to know where Claudia is," I ventured.

"You do? Soap my back, will you? It's so hard to reach."

Annabella obliged reluctantly, while I sat down beside the bath.

"Please help us," I said gently.

"It is extremely important. You must tell us all you know," Annabella insisted with a harshness which I knew instinctively would not help us reach our goal. Indeed, we were rewarded with a girlish pout.

"I am a prima ballerina," sniffed Eone Merriman. "I do not have to do anything I do not wish to."

"No, no, of course not," I soothed, stroking her hand as I glared Annabella into silence. "We're very sorry. Is there anything we can do to make amends for our rudeness?"

The almond eyes sparkled with mischief and mirth.

"Yes. You may frig me."

I tried not to show my surprise; but I must have failed, for the girl burst out laughing.

"I do declare, Miss Stanbridge, if you are a friend of Claudia's, as you say, then you must surely know how to frig a lady!"

"Well...yes. But—"

"No buts, Miss Stanbridge. Frig me directly, or I shan't tell you another thing."

What could I do but comply? To refuse would have set Eone against us; and in any case, I cannot say that the prospect of frigging her filled me with horror. On the contrary, as I slid my hand down under the surface of the foaming water, my own clitty throbbed and ached with the excitement of this unexpected encounter.

Eone leaned back in the bath, eyes closed.

"Your friend may pinch my nipples," she instructed

lazily. "She isn't so pretty as you; but since she is behind me and my eyes are closed, I shan't mind in the slightest."

Eone's maidenhead was slippery as oiled satin as I wriggled my fingers up between her thighs and into the undersea cavern of her sex. Her giggles and gasps, and ecstatic wriggles as my fingertips brushed the head of her love-button made it quite difficult to perform the task which I had been set, but the challenge had been quite clear: satisfy my whim, or you shall not have what you want.

In all honesty, it was not an onerous task. Eone Merriman was a very responsive young lady, and she seemed to offer her whole body to pleasure as though it were a starring role in a new ballet. Her suppleness, her grace, her enthusiasm were quite infectious, and I confess that I imagined how it would feel if the roles were reversed, with Eone sliding her fingers between the lobes of my sex while Annabella—perhaps rather less than enthusiastically—pinched and kneaded my breasts.

Eone climaxed with a squeal of triumph and flopped back into the bath, splashing water and flecks of lather all over the carpet. Her eyes flickered open, and a broad smile lit up her face.

"You are indeed friends of Claudia Dungarrow," she said with a wink.

"And you will tell us where she is?" demanded Annabella, who had clearly not lost sight of the practical reason for our visit.

Eone sighed. "Such impatience! Why can we not fuck and frig a little first? Then perhaps I will tell you…."

But Annabella had her by the wrists. "Now!" she said firmly. Eone wriggled sulkily free of her grasp.

"Very well. Since you insist on knowing, I have been acting as an agent for Claudia, gathering together her possessions, buying them back for her, when necessary, and sending them to her."

"Sending them to her? Where?"

Eone yawned.

"Oh, I can't remember. Somewhere…"

"You must remember! Was it anywhere near Cambridge?

Eone seemed to think this the funniest thing in the world.

"Cambridge? Heavens, no! Somewhere in France." She called out to her dresser. "Edith, come here at once, you lazy girl. Bring me my address book. Oh, and fetch a fresh jug of hot water. You have let my bath get cold again."

CHAPTER 6

From the journal of Elizabeth Stanbridge:
The journey to Dover was, to say the least, tense.

Annabella and I were beginning to feel extremely uncomfortable in each other's company. Were it not for the great peril in which poor Demelza found herself, we should doubtless have come to blows before very long. But Eone Merriman had provided us with Claudia's forwarding address in Paris, and naturally we must join forces in the hope of cornering our old enemy and saving Demelza.

Consequently, we packed our overnight bags and took the first available train to Dover. Our journey was made somewhat less unpleasant by the company of a trio of extremely pretty young ladies. I could tell by the way her eyes lingered on their fresh complexions and supple girl-ish figures that Annabella was as taken with them as I.

"Where have you travelled from?" I inquired of the eldest girl, a willowy creature with sparkling eyes and a small, pert mouth.

"From Harrogate," she replied. "My sisters and I are travelling to Milan."

"Indeed?" Annabella tucked a stray lock of hair under her feather-trimmed hat. "I studied art history in Milan. A most civilized city."

"Our mother is intent on our being properly finished," explained the Yorkshire lass. "She is sending us to Signora Mendoni's College for Young Ladies."

"How delightful!" I cried. "My own cousin Sarah was finished there!"

"Indeed? And was she happy?"

"So happy, she could not be persuaded to return to England! She lives in Turin, and works as a portrait painter. She is quite talented."

Such idle chatter helped to pass the time until the train drew into Dover Station. Alas, we had missed the last sailing of the day, which meant that Annabella and I were obliged to spend the night in the most dingy and unappealing harbourside boardinghouse. As the propri-etress had only one room available, we were forced to share the same bed—and I scarcely think either of us achieved more than an hour's sleep the whole night.

Naturally, we were not in the best of spirits at breakfast the following morning.

"If this turns out to be a wild goose chase, I shall hold you personally responsible," snapped Annabella, snatching the last slice of toast from the rack.

"Me!" I cried indignantly. "May I remind you, Annabella, that if you had taken greater care of Demelza—"

"And may I remind you, Elizabeth, that if it were not for you, my poor sister would never have come under the malign influence of that scheming bitch, Claudia Dungarrow!"

We glared at each other across the breakfast table. One or two of the other guests paused in their meal to stare and whisper behind their hands.

"You are making a spectacle of yourself, Annabella," I said coolly, spearing a bread roll with my knife. "Would you have all Dover talking about us?"

There was a look of venom in Annabella's grey eyes as she spread marmalade on her toast; but more than that. For a split second, I glimpsed a spark of unwilling desire which was more than echoed in my own shameful breast. I banished it instantly, reminding myself that our mutual suspicions and loathing rendered any thoughts of intimacy perfectly ludicrous.

"We shall take the early sailing to Boulogne." Annabella dabbed at her mouth with a napkin. "And once we are in France, we shall proceed directly to Paris."

"And then?" I inquired, partly because I was genuinely unsure of what we intended to do once we had found Claudia's address, and partly because it amused me to provoke Annabella to irritation.

"And then, naturally, we shall deal with Claudia."

"Naturally. But Annabella, how shall we deal with her? She has bested us before; she may do it again."

"She may have outwitted you, Elizabeth, but she has never got the better of me."

Despite the tension of the situation, such pompous wishful thinking sent me into fits of laughter.

"Annabella, how can you delude yourself so? Claudia ruined your reputation, had you dismissed from St. Matilda's in disgrace—"

"Claudia is a self-obsessed bitch who thinks a great deal of herself."

"And you do not?"

Annabella's swift avoidance of my gaze confirmed my suspicion: that in her secret heart, Annabella cherished certain dark fantasies about Claudia Dungarrow.

"Manifestly not."

"If Claudia is a bitch," I ventured, "she is a very clever one."

Annabella threw down her napkin. "Elizabeth, you are a perfect imbecile."

And with that, she stalked out of the dining room leaving behind a circle of startled faces.

We disembarked at Boulogne just before lunch—not that either of us cared to think much of eating, after our choppy crossing. Next, we must find the railway station and a train bound for Paris. Naturally, Annabella insisted on making use of her "excellent" French, which is not excellent at all, for Annabella's training was in the classics and nowadays few people in France speak Latin.

Nevertheless, we at last found ourselves on the correct platform and presented our tickets to the guard of the Paris train. To my dismay, he shook his head.

"Impossible, mesdemoiselles."

"What is he saying?" demanded Annabella.

"I thought you spoke faultless French!"

"Elizabeth, if you do not cease these childish games we shall miss the train!"

I sighed. There is something about Annabella which makes me want to shake her until her teeth rattle. And then fuck her until she begs for mercy…

"Monsieur," I began. *"Nous ne comprenons pas. Nous sommes anglaises. Voulez-vous expliquer, s'il vous plaît?"*

The guard proceeded to explain that we could not possibly board the train—the only Paris train for several hours—because all the carriages had been reserved by a "special and very important" passenger.

"But this is outrageous!" exclaimed Annabella. "We *must* board this train."

"Impossible," replied the guard with expressionless bureaucratic insistence.

"Do you not know who I am? I am Lady Annabella Fitzgerald!"

I was on the point of reminding Annabella that the French had guillotined their own aristocracy when one of the carriage doors opened and a lady stepped out.

A lady indeed, I thought to myself with silent awe. She was well above average height, for she towered above the guard, and shook aside his proffered steadying hand. Dressed in violet watered silk, she was dramatically, exotically beautiful, with skin as smooth and pale as marble and hair so dark that I thought it black until a ray of sun caught it, and turned the color to a rich ruby flame.

She took a few steps toward us, looked us up and down and smiled.

"*Enchantée.*"

I opened my mouth to speak, but could not find the right words. This vision of statuesque womanhood had quite taken my breath away.

"Allow me to present myself," she said, speaking now in scarcely accented English. "I am the Comtesse Florizel de Montaigne."

She offered me her hand to kiss. Almost reflexively, I bobbed a curtsy as my lips met the smooth skin, and the cool hardness of an immense canary diamond.

"Your name, child?" she inquired imperiously.

"Elizabeth. Elizabeth Stanbridge."

"Charming. Quite charming."

The Comtesse turned slowly to look at Annabella, who resolutely refused to be cowed.

"So you are Lady Annabella Fitzgerald?"

Annabella had the good manners to incline her head a fraction.

"That is correct."

"And you wish to travel to Paris?"

"It is a matter of the utmost urgency. My sister Demelza is in the greatest peril."

"I see. Well, as the guard has told you, this is my own private train. However—"

I seized the Comtesse's hand.

"If you would permit us to travel with you, we would be most grateful. Most grateful."

She stroked my hand thoughtfully, as though weighing up the precise value of our gratitude.

"Very well," she decided. "You may share my private carriage." Her smile was secretive, mysterious. "But before you embark, I should perhaps warn you that you may be a little surprised."

The interior of the Comtesse's private carriage was more than merely surprising. It was a palace for a sexual gourmet.

As the train set off with a jolt, the Comtesse observed our reactions.

"Do you like my taste in decor, Lady Annabella?" she inquired with a hint of irony. "Does it please your English sensibilities?"

Annabella's eyes ranged around the carriage walls, taking in wooden punishment frames, lashes, handcuffs, leather couches crisscrossed with straps....

"It is most...unusual." I saw her lick her lips, in the way she did when something had whetted her sensual appetite. And I confess that alarmed though I was by this new development, I, too, was rather stimulated by the sights that surrounded me.

"Unusual? But my dear Annabella, in this country, my sensual preferences are known as the English vice. Surely you are not going to disappoint me?"

Suddenly I felt my arms being wrenched behind my back. There was no time to struggle or resist. Within seconds, metal cuffs had clicked shut about my wrists.

"What are you doing? Let me go!" I cried, but the Comtesse regarded me impassively.

"You have spirit," she commented. "I believe I am going to enjoy you. Both of you."

Sweat trickled slowly down Annabella's face as the train rattled down the track, making the carriage rock gently from side to side.

"Tighter, *ma chérie?*" purred the Comtesse, twisting the ropes a little more so that they tightened about Annabella's torso, crisscrossing about her bare breasts and making them bulge out into rose-tipped white globes. She tried to wriggle, but her chains held her fast. Her arms were stretched out at shoulder height and fastened to a wooden frame, her legs spread wide so that the lobes of her sex gaped open, revealing the sweet pink flesh within.

"No more!" gasped Annabella. "No more." But I knew from the stiffness of her nipples and the quick shallowness of her breathing that Annabella was in the grip of the most terrible spasms of lust.

I could do nothing to intervene, even if I had wished to. My wrists were chained to my ankles, and I lay helpless on the carriage floor, my sex bruised and aching from the Comtesse's energetic lovemaking. In any case, why should Annabella escape paying an equal price for her fare?

The Comtesse ran her sharpened fingernails down Annabella's belly, leaving parallel tracks on the smooth white skin.

"I think you are ready now, *chérie*. Ready and willing."

The Comtesse signaled to one of her servants, the crop-haired amazon who had overwhelmed me so suddenly and unexpectedly.

"You may bring it to me now."

"The leather, madame?"

"No, no, something a little more special. The ivory, perhaps…no, the crystal. Bring it to me quickly, now, before my appetite fades."

The amazon unlocked a travelling box, and searched through furs and silks, trinkets and playthings, until she found what she was looking for: a strangely shaped object wrapped up in a length of white panne velvet.

"Here it is, madame. Shall I prepare you?"

"Naturellement, Aline. I know that my guest is as hungry for me as I am for her. Is that not so, *ma chère* Annabella?"

Annabella did not reply. Her eyes were fixed on the unrolling velvet, and the curious object which emerged from within. It was quite exquisite, a beautiful instrument of pleasure carved from a single huge rose-pink crystal— and as I set eyes upon it, I felt a pang of covetous lust. Why should Annabella, who was so very unwilling to cooperate in any of the Comtesse's games, enjoy the first kiss of this breathtakingly lovely trinket?

It was a double-ended dildo; two long, curving spikes almost as thick as a girl's wrist, one of which was attached to pink ribbons which were evidently intended to be tied about the waist and thighs.

"Do you not find this an agreeable plaything?" The Comtesse held it up for Annabella's inspection. Annabella's eyes grew wide with pretended fear, though I knew her one true emotion was excitement. Already, she was anticipating the pleasure which was about to be "forced" upon her.

"Take it away from me and untie me this instant," Annabella said quietly, with all the authority she could muster.

The Comtesse laughed. "Still playing the outraged virgin, Lady Annabella? Truly, your modesty does you credit—such a pity that the scent of your sex betrays you." She stretched out a finger and slipped it between Annabella's thighs. It came away glistening and moist. "Such a river of honeyjuice you have for me, Annabella. Really, I am quite touched. Now, Aline, prepare me."

Aline lifted her mistress's skirts and tucked them into her belt, revealing plump buttocks and a fine expanse of bare thighs. This inviting panorama was crowned by a plump and inviting pubis covered with closely clipped reddish hair, revealing inner labia which protruded slightly from between the outer lips, like the magenta tip of a lewd and mischievous tongue.

"Now the dildo," the Comtesse instructed. Aline proceeded to slide one of the curved spikes into her mistress's cunny, then attached it snugly to her body by means of the pink ribbons.

"All is ready, madame."

"And you, Annabella? You are ready to accept the pleasure we are about to share?"

Annabella had not the slightest choice in the matter, for she was spread-eagled like a starfish and could barely move a muscle.

"No! No, I won't—"

She was promptly silenced by a passionate kiss, as the Comtesse scythed into her in one swift movement, forcing their two bodies together like opposing magnetic poles. For a moment Annabella seemed to resist this sudden violation, every muscle in her body tensing and twitching, her wrists and ankles straining to burst their bonds. Then, as the Comtesse's thrusts became ever more insistent and the pleasure they gave more insidiously powerful, I saw her fall back, exhausted and defeated.

Poor dear Annabella! Forgive me one moment of amusement, for it was indeed diverting to see my haughty companion so swiftly and easily overcome, not by the Comtesse's sensual skills, but by the force of her own lustful urges. One truth at least was imparted to me by Claudia Dungarrow: hypocrisy is exposed all too easily, for it cannot long conceal an inherently sensual nature.

Ah, and it was pleasurable, too, to have the victorious Comtesse turn toward me and smile, the beautiful rose-pink dildo still strapped between her thighs. And to hear her say: "Fear not, *ma jolie Anglaise,* I have not forgotten you. It is several hours yet before we reach Paris."

When at last we bade farewell to the Comtesse, at the Gare du Nord, I felt more than a twinge of regret. Her company had proved stimulating and—paradoxically—rather liberating. Better still, it had diverted me from the necessity to spend every waking moment with Annabella Fitzgerald.

"Give me the address." Annabella seized the scrap of paper from my hand. "Summon a carriage; we must go there immediately."

I was tempted to tell her to summon it herself; but as luck would have it, a fiacre happened along at that very moment, and we clambered aboard swiftly.

"Carrefour St.-Jacques," ordered Annabella. "And make good speed."

The driver frowned in puzzlement. "Carrefour St.-Jacques? You're sure of that, mademoiselle?"

"Of course I am sure. Do you take me for a fool?"

With an expressive shrug, the cabman turned back to his horse and we set off through the streets of Paris.

"Do you suppose we shall find Claudia there when we arrive?" I wondered.

"If not, we shall wait for her. She is bound to return sooner or later."

I was less confident of the outcome, but chose not to express my doubts. Annabella was not in the mood to be contradicted.

In about half an hour, the cab came to a sudden halt in the middle of an almost-deserted crossroads.

"Why have we stopped?" Annabella demanded.

"This is it—Carrefour St.-Jacques, just as you said. That will be twenty francs."

"But—this can't be right!"

"Well it's what you said, mademoiselle, so if you'll kindly get out of my cab I'll be on my way."

I got down from the fiacre and surveyed the scene. Surely this couldn't be Claudia's address—not here. Not in the middle of nowhere. I was standing at the crossroads of two intersecting streets, quite unremarkable. In fact the only distinguishing feature about the Carrefour St.-Jacques seemed to be the equestrian statue right in the middle. I walked across and examined it, followed reluctantly by Annabella.

"This cannot be the place; the cabman must have made a mistake."

"I don't think so, Annabella. More likely this was a trick. Perhaps we have been deceived."

"No! That slut Eone Merriman was a teasing little minx, but she had not the wit to deceive anyone! I will not be played for a fool, Elizabeth!"

"It seems you may not have much choice," I replied with some spirit.

I looked at the monument in front of us. It consisted of a bronze statue of Napoleon, sitting astride his horse and pointing vaguely eastward.

"Since there is clearly no purpose in remaining here, we may as well leave," Annabella sniffed.

"Wait." I laid a hand on Annabella's arm; she shook it off.

"What is it now?"

"This inscription." I pointed to the chiselled letters in the stone plinth: "Presented to the French nation by the people of Baden-Baden."

"So?"

"Baden-Baden? That's somewhere in Germany, isn't it?"

"I believe it is. But what possible purpose…?"

I took a closer look at Napoleon. The poor man had hardly been depicted with any great sympathy. His nose was enormous, his belly hung over his breeches, and he had a wart on his chin.

"They can't have liked him much, can they? It's horrible."

"It's an excellent likeness."

"Quite."

And then something resonated in my memory. Something which connected Claudia Dungarrow with Baden-Baden. Something that made my stomach turn over.

"No!"

"Whatever is the matter, Elizabeth?"

I seized Annabella's hands and looked into her eyes.

"Fräulein Schleiss," I whispered. "Fräulein Irmgard Schleiss!"

From the journal of Claudia Dungarrow:
Eone Merriman purred and mewed with pleasure. Small wonder, since she was lying naked on my tiger-skin rug with her pretty little arse in the air and her admirably tight pussy completely at my mercy.

"Oh Claudia," she whispered, giggling and writhing as I set about her arsecheeks with an oiled leather paddle. "Mistress Claudia, have I been a very bad girl?"

"On the contrary, you have been an especially good slut, which is why I am rewarding you with such a delicious punishment."

97

"Ah. Oh!" she cried out as I brought down the paddle on her upturned backside. "Oh, Mistress, it tingles so. My bottom feels as if it is on fire!"

"And does the beating also stimulate other parts of you, my wicked little slut?"

"Yes, yes, Mistress! My clitty—oh, my clitty, it burns and throbs. I can scarcely keep myself from coming."

"But you must, dear slut. You must. Until such time as I tell you that you can come."

And just to make her ordeal a more testing one, I threw down the paddle and proceeded to slide my curled fist into her smoothly lubricated sex. I smiled.

"They took the bait, my dear slut. Hook, line, and sinker. Soon they will be in Baden-Baden."

Eone giggled and squirmed. "Oh Mistress Claudia, you are so clever! So much cleverer than I could ever be."

"Indeed." It occurred to me that this was no great compliment. I twisted my fist round and round and from side to side in a corkscrew motion, stretching the walls of Eone's sex.

"But, Mistress—"

"What, slut?"

"Is it not a little…cruel? To send them to Irmgard Schleiss? She is so very…"

"Very what, Eone?"

"Very severe."

"Is that so, slut?" Sliding my other hand between Eone's legs, I sought out her clitoris and pinched it very hard, ensuring that she enjoyed the full benefit of my fingernails. "More severe than your Mistress Claudia?"

Eone sighed and climaxed, her sex quivering and throbbing about my fist.

"Ah no, Mistress Claudia," she murmured as she sank onto her belly on the tiger-skin rug. "No one could ever be as wonderfully severe as you."

CHAPTER 7

From the journal of Elizabeth Stanbridge:
The train moved slowly across France, heading toward the distant border with Germany.

Annabella had secured beds for us on the overnight train, but alas there were no individual berths. We were forced to share a two-bedded compartment scarcely bigger than a wardrobe. Small wonder that, although not particularly hungry, we were both eager to repair to the dining car for the evening meal. At least there we would escape the claustrophobic proximity which was rapidly fraying our nerves.

"We shall require separate tables," declared Annabella, preceding me into the dining car. I had no dispute with this arrangement; but, as luck would have it, only one empty table remained.

"You will not object to dining together, mesdemoiselles?" The waiter indicated the small corner table, set with a crisp white cloth and two place settings. Annabella's mouth set in a curl of displeasure.

"So. It seems that even here I am not free of your company, Elizabeth."

"It pleases me no more than it pleases you," I replied with as much calm as I could muster. "But what is the point of fretting so? You will merely give yourself indigestion."

We sat down at the table directly opposite each other and perused the menu. Or at least, that is what we tried to do. But our eyes would keep creeping up over the top of the menus, making the briefest of contact then darting away, as though denying that they had the slightest desire to look at each other.

"The escalope of chicken, lightly grilled. Fresh strawberries and a glass of Madeira wine." Annabella handed back her menu and, without a glance at me, added, "Miss Stanbridge will have the same."

My jaw dropped. The arrogance of the woman!

"I will not," I declared. "I will have Wiener schnitzel with noodles and sauerkraut. And a glass of weissbier."

Annabella sneered her disapproval. "And that is a recipe for sound digestion? Really, Elizabeth, will you never learn to be guided by your betters?"

"I am quite capable of making my own choices, thank you very much," I snapped back.

We ate in silence, punctuated by the occasional request for salt or another glass of water. But our studied indifference was too self-conscious to be genuine. With every morsel of food which passed my lips, I became more and more aware of Annabella, the closeness of her, the animal scent of her body....

Beneath the table, I shifted my foot slightly and made unexpected contact with Annabella's silk-stockinged ankle. The touch lasted scarcely more than a few seconds and could scarcely be described as a caress, yet it seemed to send electric shivers through my body, and I knew from the quiver of Annabella's lips that she could feel it, too.

Then she drew her foot away angrily.

"Keep to your side of the table, Elizabeth! I will not have you taking liberties with my person."

"You flatter yourself, Annabella. I have not the slightest desire to do anything of the kind."

But it was a lie, and we both knew it. The musky scent of my own desire, stronger now than the eau de cologne I had dabbed on my temples and in the valley between my breasts, seemed to fill my nostrils. Could Annabella smell it too, as I could smell the unmistakable perfume of her need?

As I sipped iced tea, I tried to banish the wicked images which entered my head unbidden. Images of

Annabella naked, memories of the cool firmness of her flesh as we had lain sleepless in the same bed in our Dover boardinghouse. Questions, too: what was she wearing beneath that sensible gown of grey muslin? Gauzy underthings, or sensible drawers of crisp white linen? Were her breasts as firm and luscious to kiss as I remembered them?

Shame on you Elizabeth Stanbridge, I scolded myself. How could you admit such thoughts, when Annabella Fitzgerald has never harbored anything but hostility toward you, and has even sought to part you from your own dear Demelza!

But fate was moving swiftly, and little did I suspect that soon our deeper, darker urges would be beyond our control.

After dinner, we returned reluctantly to our sleeping quarters.

"It is late," I commented. "I shall retire to bed."

Perhaps once asleep, I should be able to escape these tormenting fantasies about Annabella. I selected the lower bunk and laid my overnight case upon it.

"What are you doing, Elizabeth?" Annabella demanded.

"Preparing for bed—what else?"

"Yours is the upper berth."

"Indeed? And when was this decided?"

"You cannot expect me to climb a ladder like some circus monkey!"

"But it is acceptable for me—is that it?"

"Don't be such a peevish child, Elizabeth."

"I shall perhaps cease to be peevish when you cease to be an overbearing and insufferable harridan!"

I knew instantly that I had gone too far. Annabella's eyes flashed like smoke-grey diamonds and she lashed out, striking me with a hard slap across the cheek which brought the sting of tears to my eyes.

"How dare you speak to me like that!"

Hand clasped to my cheek, I stood my ground.

"I shall speak to you exactly as I wish."

Annabella's response was to seize me by my hair and twist it, so hard that the pins flew out in all directions and I was forced onto my belly on the bunk in my attempt to escape the pain.

"Get off me, get off me!" I snarled, kicking back like an enraged mule—to such fortunate effect that the high heel of my shoe caught Annabella's shin. She leapt back with curses of pain.

"You little vixen!"

I did not waste the moment's advantage which I had been given. Recovering my strength, I sprang at Annabella and pushed her hard, catching her off-balance and sending her sprawling onto her backside.

But Annabella is stronger and heavier than I, and instinctively I knew that my victory would be short-lived. A moment later, she had me in her grasp and was pulling me down on top of her.

"Let go of me!" I sank my teeth into Annabella's

hand, but she would not relax her grip on me, not even for a moment.

"I'll teach you to defy me, you worthless little trollop."

Her strong fingers tore at the buttons on my dress and ripped open the bodice, exposing my stays. My breasts were hers to possess, for they were scarcely veiled at all by the boned corset, which pushed and lifted them, shaping them into plump and tempting pink-stalked apples.

Annabella's tongue slid between my breasts and described broad, wet circles around my nipples, awakening my unwilling desire yet not making the slightest attempt to satisfy it.

"No!" I cried as I struggled in her grasp, ripping at her gown and pulling the choker from her throat, sending pearls cascading all over the juddering carriage floor.

"You clumsy slut! I'll make you pay for that!"

I responded by spitting in Annabella's face, summoning up all the fury and loathing in my soul.

"So make me!"

I dug my knee into Annabella's belly and slid it down in a savage knife-thrust, so that it dived between her legs and my thigh fetched up against her pussy, warm and yielding beneath her gown. Annabella let out a quavering sob of angry pleasure, her face contorting in rage at her own weakness.

But I had underestimated her. Scant moments later, she had me on my back on the carriage floor, my gown ripped from my body and my drawers pulled down to my ankles.

"You stink of sex!" hissed Annabella, plunging her index finger into my sex and making me writhe with shame. "What filthy thoughts are in that festering brain of yours, Elizabeth? What seeds of sensual corruption has Claudia sown within you?"

"The same that she has planted within you," I replied softly, triumphant even in defeat. For Annabella might be physically stronger than I, but she was no less a creature of base and sensual appetites.

"How dare you!"

"I dare because it is true. And you know it, Annabella Fitzgerald. You are as much a creation of Claudia Dungarrow as I am!"

Retribution for this reckless outburst was as swift as it was predictable. Shrieking so loudly that I feared she would bring the whole train rushing to our compartment, she threw me onto my belly and forced apart my buttocks.

I resisted, of course. But a part of me rebelled, for the desire in me was so strong. And when Annabella's fist forced its way between my arsecheeks, ecstasy mingled with my anger and my shame.

The following morning, I awoke in the top berth; this was one victory which I had decided to cede to Annabella. If she believed herself to be my mistress and my superior in all things, then I was happy to allow her that belief—but she was deluding herself if she expected any display of loyalty from me.

I rolled onto my belly and looked out through the window. The train braked, and the countryside began to clatter past more slowly.

"We are coming to the German border," said Annabella, who was already dressed and completing her toilette at the mirror. "You had better make yourself decent; I have heard that the guards make very thorough inspections."

In this respect, at least, Annabella was not mistaken. I had not been dressed five minutes when we drew into the station and I looked out to see hordes of uniformed German guards stalking about on the platform, full of their own importance.

It was then that we heard the sound of running feet in the corridor outside.

"What—" I began, but did not succeed in finishing my sentence, for there came a furious knocking on the door of our compartment.

"Do not open it," said Annabella. "It is bound to be someone up to no good, a fugitive from justice."

Ignoring Annabella's demand, I opened the door, and was astounded when I was almost knocked flying by a young African woman, smartly dressed but disheveled and extremely distressed.

"*Aidez-moi, je vous en prie!*" she exclaimed in faultless French.

"Throw her out," said Annabella.

I took the young stranger by the arm and drew her into the compartment.

"Whatever is the matter?" I asked her.

Tears sprang to the young woman's eyes, and she wiped them away with the back of her hand.

"My husband…save me, *je vous en prie!* Save me from him!"

"Your husband?" Annabella came forward to inspect the stranger, evidently deciding that since she could not simply dismiss her, she had better take charge instead. "What of him?"

The young woman clasped her hands.

"Please, please don't send me away. If you don't hide me from the guards they will send me back. Back…to him…"

"To your husband? He is cruel to you?"

She nodded, her tears flowing freely now.

"He beats me, because I…because I will not…" She cast down her eyes, her whole body trembling. "All men are repugnant to me, mademoiselle."

Annabella and I exchanged glances. For once, at least, we were united in our response.

"Of course we shall hide you," I told the young woman. "Now, what is your name?"

"Marie-Jeanne Dupont, mademoiselle."

"Calm yourself, Marie-Jeanne. We shall find a way of helping you."

"Naturally we cannot abandon one of our Sapphic sisters to such...barbarous treatment," Annabella agreed. "Quickly child, hide yourself in the wardrobe, behind my evening gowns."

And so we found ourselves accomplices to a most attractive fugitive, despite our better judgment—for, as Annabella had predicted, the German border guards were extremely thorough. Indeed, they might have prolonged their search of our compartment, had they not been confronted with a scene which sent them scuttling away, pale-faced and horror-stricken.

Ah, dear reader. How amusing it is to contemplate the arrogant sexuality of men. I shall never forget the looks on the guards' faces when they entered our compartment and found Annabella reclining on the bed, her thighs spread wide and my tongue thrust deep inside her gloriously naked pussy.

I was rather sad to take leave of the lissome Marie-Jeanne. Annabella and I had spent several most agreeable hours in her company, and she demonstrated a gift for gamahuching which is certain to find her a staunch protectress wherever she seeks her fortune.

But we had done our duty by our pretty fugitive, and must not lose sight of our quest: to seek out Claudia and free Demelza from her clutches.

Afternoon was fading into evening when our train reached the spa town of Baden-Baden, a fashionable resort among the titled, wealthy, tubercular, and neurotic. The town nestles quite prettily among the fir-covered hills of the Rhine Valley, with a fine view to the northeast and Merkur Mountain.

One might have frittered away many an idle hour in Baden-Baden, rubbing shoulders with the Grand-Duchess Marie-Louise of Prussia, listening to the orchestra in the Kurgarten, taking the waters, or prome-nading in the twilight and observing the host of lovely young girls. But Annabella and I were here for a purpose which transcended the purely recreational.

After taking a room at the Hotel Messmer, we refreshed ourselves with a light supper.

"We must seek out Fräulein Schleiss," I ventured, giving voice to the dread thought which had been in both our minds ever since that terrible moment in Paris.

"Indeed."

"We could wait until tomorrow…"

Annabella shook her head, rising to her feet and smoothing the creases from her gown.

"We shall go tonight. For Demelza's sake."

My footsteps felt leaden as we walked through the twilit streets of Baden-Baden. The gas lamps were just beginning to be lit, and the air was warm and dusky-blue. It would have been a perfect evening to take an innocent stroll, but we were headed toward Königstrasse, and the house of Fräulein Irmgard Schleiss.

Too soon we found the place: a well-to-do but unremarkable boulevard, lined with linden trees which stood before three-story houses of identical aspect. Who could have imagined that behind one of these ordinary facades lurked the far from ordinary residence of a woman whose mere reputation struck terror into my heart?

Number forty-two. It stood just before the corner of the street, overlooking a small enclosed garden and an ornamental fountain. It was Annabella who took the first step up to the door and sounded the bell.

When the door swung inward, it revealed nothing but a dimly lit passageway, with not a soul in sight. Annabella made to step inside.

"No, wait!"

She smiled grimly. "What is there to wait for? Come, Elizabeth—unless, of course, you are too afraid…?"

This was sufficient to make me follow Annabella into the house. It took a few moments for my eyes to become accustomed to the hissing yellowish light from the gas lamps, which had been turned down so low that they scarcely did more than soften the darkness.

"Where is everyone?" I inquired out loud. At that moment, a gust of wind caught the front door and flung it shut, plunging us into even greater confusion.

Then I heard the sound of footsteps on the staircase; and, looking upward, I saw the figure of a woman descending the stairs.

She was neither exceptionally tall nor heavily built,

yet her presence was so imposing that I shrank back against the wall, my whole body chilling as the cold dampness of the plaster sank into my flesh.

"Guten Abend," said Fräulein Schleiss, her black skirts swishing as she approached. Her flaxen hair gleamed like spun glass in the light from the lantern she carried. Fantastical shadows danced about her in the gloom.

"Welcome, dear ladies. Welcome to the House of Pain."

CHAPTER 8

Never, even in my dreams, had I imagined any place as strange and as terrible as the House of Pain.

As Fräulein Schleiss led us through the house, I discovered quickly that it was far from deserted. Naked women writhed in the shadows, some chained to the walls, others hobbled or bound into lewd and unnatural postures. Some of their bodies were striped with red welts or dotted with teeth marks and bruises. Some were decorated with piercings and tattoos, the like of which I have never seen in any other place.

"Do you like my pets?" inquired Fräulein Schleiss. "Their suffering is my masterpiece: my great, defining work of art."

"Your…pets?"

I felt something touch the toe of my boot and looked down. At first I thought I had fallen into some nightmare or some inner pit of Hell, for the creature at my feet possessed two heads and four arms. Then I saw that twin Chinese girls had been bound together, breast to back, so that as one girl crawled on all fours she bore her sister on her back. Their hands moved incessantly, clawing and caressing, seeking pleasure which was denied to them by the iron chastity harness which encased their two-fold sex.

"Give," mouthed one of the girls, putting out her tongue and licking my boot. "Give. Pleasure. Give."

"Get away from me!"

With a shudder I stepped back; but Irmgard Schleiss dealt with her "pets" more severely, seizing a whip from the wall and administering six stinging lashes across the mass of naked flesh before her. The two girls moaned and sobbed, each stroke seeming to intensify their pleasure; until, at the last stroke, they screeched in ecstasy and fell squirming to the floor, exhausted by their own depravity.

Irmgard Schleiss fixed her gaze upon me.

"You are shocked by my little pets and their taste for punishment?"

My voice trembled as I replied, "It is not for me to question another's means of obtaining pleasure."

"Ah. But is that pleasure also yours?"

"I—"

Fräulein Schleiss's face moved very close to mine, her eyes searching for any sign of weakness. "Do you like to give pain or receive it, Fräulein Elizabeth?"

Without waiting for a reply, she turned to Annabella.

"You are a giver of pain, are you not?"

Annabella feigned bravado, but the tip of her tongue flicked nervously across her lips.

"A dispenser of discipline, perhaps…where it is appropriate."

Fräulein Schleiss shook her head. "It is useless lying to me, Annabella. I sensed the depths of your soul the moment I set eyes on you. You like to believe that you are a giver of pain, a connoisseur of others' suffering; but that is not your true pleasure, Annabella. Not your true pleasure at all." She beckoned to us. "Follow."

We were standing before a heavy wooden door. Taking a large key from her belt, she unlocked it and motioned to us to step inside. As the key turned in the lock behind us, I feared that we had made a terrible mistake—but it was too late to turn back now.

The room in which we now stood had been converted, perhaps from an elegant salon, into the perfect punishment chamber: a dungeon in which every form of sensual cruelty might be explored. A rack, an iron maiden, weights and straps, whips and blades; everywhere I looked I saw some new and ingenious means of inflicting torment.

"I see that you are impressed by my toys," Irmgard Schleiss commented. "Allow me to demonstrate their use to you."

Annabella cut in, "We have not come here for such things. We have come because you know the where-abouts of Dr. Claudia Dungarrow."

"Perhaps. Perhaps not. But let me tell you, Lady Annabella, those who come here do not demand. They do not even ask. They beg."

Fear touched my heart. Something told me that Fräulein Schleiss's words were far from empty. All at once I wanted to turn tail and run away, to smash my way through the locked door and disappear into the night.

"I have a proposition to put to you," said Fräulein Schleiss. "A game, if you like." She stroked my chin, tilting it suddenly so that I was forced to look into her eyes. "You like games, don't you, my pretty one?"

"What game is this?" Annabella demanded. "And what do you know of Claudia Dungarrow?"

"A game of...endurance. I have something you want—certain information regarding Claudia, but I cannot simply give it to you, can I? That would be far too easy. Too easy by far, my dear ones."

She slid a sealed envelope out of her pocket, walked across to a cabinet, and locked it inside.

"Inside that envelope is the information you crave. If you want it, you must earn it. And to earn it, you must submit yourselves to an ordeal of my choosing. An ordeal of exquisite pain."

Mistress Claudia had taught me that in the midst of pain there can be great pleasure. She schooled me also in the ways of endurance and submission. Without her tutelage, I could not have hoped to withstand the onslaught of Fräulein Schleiss's sensual armory.

The punishment room was thick-walled, carefully designed not to allow any of the sounds of torment to escape. Within its walls Annabella and I were utterly alone, abandoned to the ungentle mercies of the Mistress of Pain. To be sure, we could simply have declined her challenge and left the house forever, but without the information she offered, how could we ever hope to track Claudia down?

The rope about my wrists jerked tight, and my feet lifted off the floor, suspending me like a trussed fly from the ceiling. I would have cried out, but doing so would have meant failure: the challenge of pain is to endure in absolute silence, to the very point of agony or orgasm. And beyond.

"Good girl," purred Fräulein Schleiss. "You are more resilient than I had given you credit for." She turned to one of her flunkies, a masked girl clad from head to foot in skintight rubber. "Lift her higher. She must not touch the floor even with the tips of her toes."

My arms felt as though they were being wrenched

from their sockets, and my whole body seemed to be straining to tear itself apart. For the cruel witch had attached iron cuffs about my thighs, linked to chains bolted to the ceiling; so that whenever the chains were tightened, my thighs were jerked apart.

I bit my lip to stifle a cry as my legs were pulled wider and wider apart, exposing every secret of my sex: the sweet, glistening ruby fruit of my cunny and the amber furrow leading to the discreetly puckered kiss of my anus.

"Now, dear child, where to begin—that is the question." There was a world of sweet malevolence in her voice. "Where to begin... Ah, yes, my dear, your darling holes. They are so very tight. Let us see how greedy they are."

I did not understand what she meant, until I felt the first of the cold metal balls pushing its way into my vagina. Each was about the size of a billiard ball, very smooth and heavy, and Fräulein Schleiss pushed in one after the other: two, three, five, six—where would it end? When she began forcing still more of the silver balls into my anus, my body began to shake with the sheer effort of containing them within me.

"You must not let them fall, sweet child," Fräulein Schleiss whispered. "You must keep them inside you; if you let a single one fall, you shall forfeit the challenge."

My muscles ached with the terrible effort of holding onto the balls. Worse, they were moving about inside me, provoking sensations which were at once pleasurable and tormenting. Slippery juices were coursing out of me, lubricating the balls and making them almost impossible to grip. Only by the most agonizing effort of muscle control did I succeed in enduring, all the time praying that the ordeal would soon be over.

Meanwhile, Annabella was not faring any more gently. The Teutonic dominatrix had her bound to an upright frame, with a crossbar about five feet off the ground. Annabella's buttocks were balanced on the bar, her knees apart and chained to the uprights, whilst her head was hanging forward and attached by loose chains to her wrists and ankles. A further chain passed between her legs and was jerked hard into the soft flesh of her pussy whenever she lost her balance or used her hands to steady herself.

"I do hope you are not too comfortable," Fräulein Schleiss said softly, clicking her fingers to summon her silent servant. The masked girl stepped forward, carrying a velvet cushion on which were laid five different instruments of torture. "I would not wish to deprive you of the suffering which your companion is currently enjoying."

I watched as she selected her chosen instrument: a cat-o'-nine-tails with an inlaid silver handle and soft chamois leather thongs, tipped with cruel spikes of lead shot.

"Now let us see if you have dear sweet Elizabeth's

resilience," she purred; and in the same breath let fly the lash on Annabella's well-rounded backside.

To her credit, Annabella did not cry out, even though the force of the blow left red marks all over her flesh and almost made her topple forward, causing the chain to dig deep into the softness of her pussy.

"Good girl. And again. Again. Again." The words were punctuated by the flash of Fräulein Schleiss's arm, bringing down the lash upon Annabella's flesh. Each blow seemed harder than the last, reddening the flesh, drawing crimson beads of blood, threatening to make Annabella lose her balance and cry out in pain and fear. But, though she trembled and shuddered, she let not one sound escape from between her lips.

When Fräulein Schleiss dropped the lash, for a moment I began to believe that our ordeal was over. Then I saw her open a small ivory box and take out a long needle-sharp spike.

Fear ran cold fingers down my spine. What was she going to do? What terrible pain was to be inflicted upon me now, far worse than the torment I was now enduring? But at the last moment she turned aside, and I saw that she was addressing her attentions once more to Annabella.

"See this needle, Annabella?" She held it up so that Annabella could see it clearly. It was at least six inches long, quite thick and very sharp. "It is a very special needle. You should consider yourself honoured." Fräulein Schleiss ran her finger lovingly along the metal spike. "I had considered testing your endurance by branding you with my mark, but no. That is such a coarse and unsatisfying process. Instead, I have decided to pierce you."

It was only when I saw her hand slide between Annabella's thighs that I realized exactly what Fräulein Schleiss intended, the full dreadfulness of her act. She intended to pierce Annabella through her clitty!

As the needle struck home, I had to turn my head away, certain of the scream of agony which would echo around the dungeon walls. But I was mistaken, for Annabella made no sound. When I looked back, I saw that she had swooned clean away, but Fräulein Schleiss was wearing the smile of a Cheshire cat; for great drops of pleasure-juice were falling like nectar from Annabella's wounded pussy, plashing gently onto the floor beneath her.

"Dear Annabella," murmured Fräulein Schleiss, sliding her finger into Annabella's pussy and licking off the sticky sweetness. "You really must learn to trust my judgment. For you, my dear, pain will always be more delightful to receive than to give."

I fear I must have lost consciousness, for when next I came to my senses I was lying on a bed next to Annabella, a black silk sheet softly drawn over our naked bodies and our clothes folded neatly on a chair.

And propped up on the bedside table, a sealed white envelope.

The message within the envelope proved to be not so much informative as baffling.

"This is not the address we were promised by Fräulein Schleiss!" Annabella exclaimed in high dudgeon.

"Fräulein Schleiss promised us nothing," I reminded her. "Only taunted and tantalized. We should be grateful that we have anything at all from this sorry encounter."

The "message" took the form of a picture: a small chromolithograph depicting a crowned eagle, astride a river. Upon its chest the eagle bore the letter "V."

I pondered aloud, "Whatever can it mean?"

Annabella peered over my shoulder. "It is perfectly obvious," she declared.

"It is? I cannot make anything of it."

"Of course you cannot. You are a silly featherbrained slut." I glared at Annabella, but she affected not to notice. "This message tells us to proceed to Vienna."

"You are quite sure of that?"

Annabella did not even dignify my question with a response, but began immediately to dress.

"Do hurry up, Elizabeth, or we shall miss the night train to Vienna," she snapped.

For my part, I harbored severe doubts about Annabella's analysis of the picture. But since I could come up with no better solution, I set to and prepared myself, praying silently that I was mistaken, and that in Vienna we would find both Claudia and the means to overcome her.

Our journey by train took us through the dark expanses of the Black Forest. Much to Annabella's horror, all the sleeping accommodations had already been reserved, and we found ourselves obliged to share a goods wagon with a jumble of trunks and boxes.

As the train rattled on through the night, Annabella and I did our best to ignore each other. But the night was cold, and we were forced to huddle together for warmth, flesh against flesh beneath Annabella's fur-lined cloak.

There was no moon, and darkness crept stealthily around us, hiding us from prying eyes. None witnessed the shameful lust with which my hand slipped inside Annabella's corsage, seeking out the hard swell of her breast and the secret warmth which pulsed within.

Annabella did not speak or push me away. I heard her let out a long, low sigh, and felt her flesh begin to quiver and tremble at my caress. I confess it was not tenderness which drove me to seduce her, but a lustful desire for revenge; for she had subdued me once, but I was not her plaything. I would have her. I would force her to acknowledge me as her equal. I would not become her slave.

To my surprise, she yielded readily to my kisses. My mouth upon hers, I embraced her and lowered her to the dusty carriage floor. What strange impulse had entered Annabella's soul and weakened her resolve? Had cold and weariness broken her spirit temporarily?

Had her desire for me grown too intense to suppress, fueled by her jealousy of my love for Demelza?

My thigh eased itself between her thighs, pressing up under her skirts and seeking out the moist heat of her pleasure. The skin of her arms and legs was marble-cold, but at the apex of her sex she was tropical-hot and oozing with a warm dew which had completely soaked the crotch of her drawers. She trembled convulsively as I began working my thigh back and forth in her sweet valley, forcing the pleasure from her with a rhythmic sawing motion which echoed the movement of the carriage.

Annabella, oh, Annabella. Could you feel how I trembled, also, as I stoked the secret fire of your sex? Could you divine the depth of my desire, the angry ecstasy which throbbed through me as my fingers slipped through the vent in my drawers and dipped themselves deep into my own honeypot?

I had enough self-control left to ensure that you surrendered yourself to me utterly, writhing and moaning helplessly in the grip of ruthless pleasure, before allowing myself the gratification of release. The physical satisfaction was nothing compared to the pleasure of knowing that I had earned one small victory over my old adversary.

The following morning, naturally, all had changed. Annabella acted as though nothing in the least untoward had occurred, and if anything, behaved even more dictatorially than usual toward me.

"Did you sleep well?" I inquired with seeming innocence.

"What business is that of yours?" Annabella demanded spikily.

"Only that your sleep seemed a little…disturbed." Mischief had caught hold of me, and I could not resist taunting her, just a little. I was still savoring my small victory. "I swear I heard you calling out and sighing, almost as though you were in the grip of some sweet pain…."

Annabella turned her back on me, but she could not conceal her discomfiture.

"We shall be in Vienna by noon," she said. "By tomorrow we shall have outwitted Claudia Dungarrow, and we shall be free to go our separate ways."

"You really believe that is true?"

"I must believe it, lest the prospect of spending any further time in your company reduces me to despair," Annabella replied.

Annabella was in no way cheered to discover that I had been right all along: Vienna was not the answer to the riddle. We must have walked twice round the city and looked at every bridge for miles, but nowhere did we find any sign of Claudia's presence.

But a fortuitous meeting with three ladies in a coffee-house was to set us upon a quite different course.

"You are in Vienna for the summer?" inquired one of

the ladies, who was in her early thirties and unusually comely: her flaming red hair complementing green eyes and a sprinkling of pale-gold freckles.

"Only for a few days," I replied. "We are looking for someone."

"A friend," cut in Annabella with a rather forced smile. "Her name is Dr. Claudia Dungarrow."

The three ladies exchanged shrugs. No trace of recognition appeared on their faces.

"She lives in the city?" inquired the red-haired lady's companion, a blonde with a very full red-lipped mouth and pale blue eyes.

"No. But we had been led to believe she might be here." Annabella produced the picture from her purse and laid it flat on the table. "Does this mean anything to you?"

"Heavens, a puzzle!" exclaimed the blonde delightedly. "How intriguing! Clothilde, can you think of any other cities that begin with the letter V?"

"Not one," replied the red-haired lady.

"But I can!" declared the third lady, who up to now had scarcely uttered a word. All eyes fell upon her.

"Well?" demanded Clothilde. "What is it?"

"The Vatican—V for Vatican. It seems to me that you must take yourselves to Rome if you wish to find your friend."

Dear reader, imagine our dismay at the prospect of yet another journey, toiling ever-deeper into the heart of Europe with nothing but a picture to guide us. Had it not been for the thought of poor Demelza, lying helpless in her bed at the Hall, I would have given up the quest instantly. For I had not the slightest desire to set eyes upon Claudia again—and Annabella's company was becoming very far from congenial.

The journey to Rome was accomplished in a matter of several days, somewhat hampered by a landslide which had blocked part of the railway line, obliging us to travel part of the way in a rickety farm-cart. After such discomforts, it was indeed with joy that we first set eyes upon the Eternal City.

"Wherever shall we find a place to stay?" I wondered.

"We shall be staying in Vatican City itself. I have certain friends in the city, acquaintances from the days when I came to Italy to study art and the classics."

And such "acquaintances" they proved to be, dear reader! For it was not to an hotel or private house that our coachman took us, but to the doors of a convent!

"Welcome," smiled the nun who ushered us inside. "You are most welcome to our Convent of Sisterly Love."

Exhausted after our long and unrewarding journey, we were delighted to find hot baths and warm, soft towels awaiting us in the great marble-lined bath-house. Sister Rosaria and Sister Dolorosa attended to our every need as we bathed, salving our travel-weary skin with sweet oils and afterward massaging our tired backs and shoulders with a gentle skill which quickly turned the ache of tension to the warm swell of pleasure.

I felt my whole body relax as Sister Rosaria's fingers smoothed down my limbs from shoulder blade to thigh. The sensations were smooth and subtle, her fingertips skating over my skin on a fine film of lavender and orange oil. I sighed with delight as she rolled me onto my back and began dripping warm oil onto my belly.

"You have come seeking repose and respite from the cares of the world? You have chosen well, for in this place, we are blessed with all the joys of sensual pleasure and intimate discipline."

"We have come not for ourselves but for the sake of our friend," I explained, doing my best to concentrate on our quest as Sister Rosaria blended the oil into my skin, her hands circling my aching, hardening breasts.

"Your friend?"

"My sister Demelza," explained Annabella, who was lying on her belly, her chin propped on her folded arms, as Sister Dolorosa anointed her hips and buttocks with oil of geranium. "She lies gravely ill in England. It is vital that we find a certain person…"

"Claudia Dungarrow."

Sister Dolorosa left off massaging Annabella's buttocks, her hands shimmering with a gloss of oil as they rested upon the taut flesh, her thumbs disappearing into the deep cleft of her backside.

"Dr. Claudia Dungarrow?"

"You know her?"

"Why of course!" Sister Dolorosa's cheeks reddened

slightly and she looked down, recommencing her attentions on Annabella's backside. "She is...how may I say..."

"She is a patroness of our Order," cut in Sister Rosaria, clearly the more brazen of the two, for her creamy complexion displayed not the faintest trace of a blush. "Claudia has taught us a great deal about the merits of self-discipline."

This I could well imagine. Whatever else she may be, Claudia Dungarrow is the strictest and most thorough of teachers.

"She is here?" I demanded, quivering with barely controlled pleasure as Sister Rosaria's fingers slipped suddenly between my thighs.

Sister Rosaria shook her head. "Why, no, madam. If Claudia were in Rome we should surely know it, for her fame has spread far and wide, and she would not fail to contact us."

The sensations were perfectly intolerable as Sister Rosaria's long and slender fingertips skated into the warm wetland of my sex, again and again brushing infinitely close to the hardening bud which nestled within. But I knew that I must not lose control, for Demelza's life and fate were at stake.

I sighed. "If she is not here, then wherever can she be?"

Annabella pushed away Sister Dolorosa's hand.

"Open my travelling bag. There is something inside, a small picture."

"This, madam?"

"Indeed. Bring it to me."

My head whirled. I was sinking faster and faster into a deep whirlpool of uncontrolled sensations. In truth I could scarcely make sense of anything Annabella was saying. She seemed to be talking to herself.

"Of course, of course, that must be it!"

"Annabella?"

"Why did I not think of it before? The letter is not simply the letter 'V,' it is the Roman numeral for five."

Escaping only by a tremendous effort of will from Sister Rosaria's ministering hands, I forced myself to listen.

"Annabella, I do not understand! What is this all about?"

She gave an impatient sigh.

"The Roman numeral five, Elizabeth. In the picture. It represents the fifth century A.D. That was the century in which Rome was overrun by barbarians—as you would know if you had gleaned anything of value from your expensive education."

"But what significance could that have, Annabella?"

"From the fifth century onward, Rome was no longer the center of the Roman Empire. Only the Eastern Empire remained as a beacon of classical culture. And even you, Elizabeth, must know where the Eastern Empire was ruled from."

"Constantinople," I mouthed, scarcely believing what I was saying.

"Precisely, Elizabeth. Or Istanbul, to give it its modern name. I am relieved to discover that you are not a complete ignoramus after all."

CHAPTER 9

From the journal of Claudia Dungarrow:
Ah, my dear pets. How it gratifies me to play with your puny minds and your delicious bodies. And how uselessly you struggle to resist my will, to understand the meaning hidden in my messages to you. And not once have you summoned up the courage or the wit to refuse the lure.

Before me on the table is an hourglass, fully two feet tall, the case fashioned from carved wood inlaid with mother-of-pearl. But it is not the beauty of the craftsmanship which compels my attention, it is the seductively slow trickle of the sand, falling in a fine stream to the bottom of the glass.

So little time left, my dear Elizabeth and my darling Annabella. So very little time, and where are you? Surely the clue I have given you could not be so very difficult to solve!

Laughter overtakes me, and in a wild sweep of my arm I strike the hourglass, sending it crashing to the floor. As it falls onto the tiles, the glass shatters and the sand flies out, forming strange hieroglyphic patterns.

Bending down, I pick up the remains of the hourglass, seizing it with deliberate savagery so that the jagged edge of the glass slices deep into the flesh of my palm and blood drips from the wound into the sand at my feet.

Ah, delicious pain, beautiful agony. What greater pleasure can there be in the entire world than the glory of pain? But the secret, my dear pets, lies in learning to control it: a lesson which, as yet, you are very far from learning.

Beautiful, exquisite, consummate pain. But nothing like the pain that is owing to you, my dearest darling sluts.

From the journal of Elizabeth Stanbridge:
Time was against us, yet exhaustion had laid its fell hand upon us and we could go no further without repose.

In three days we reached the Aegean coast, and at this point we were obliged to rest, for there would be no ferry to convey us for at least two more days.

"It is too bad," Annabella declared.

"It is indeed regrettable, but what purpose is there in railing against fate? What can we do but be patient?"

"Patient! How can I be patient when Demelza...?"

"I know." A quiet sorrow seemed to unite us in that moment, and for a few seconds we stood close together, my hand upon Annabella's, my cheek brushing hers; sharing not only our thoughts of Demelza, but the secret, shameful understanding of our attraction to each other.

It seemed that we were doomed to three days of enforced idleness. But as luck would have it, a local girl directed us to a secluded cove, so wild and beautiful that Sappho herself might have composed her songs of love there.

"It is so very hot, and the sea is so very blue. Shall we swim?"

"Well..." Annabella sounded doubtful, but I had set my heart upon it.

"I shall swim to that little island and back." I pointed to a tiny islet, little more than a sandbank dotted with trees, lying a few hundred yards offshore. "You may join me if you wish, if you don't I couldn't care less."

Perhaps it was the warmth of the Mediterranean sun which had relaxed our bodies and broken down the barriers of our mutual suspicion. Perhaps it was merely my pretended indifference which spurred Annabella on, but we both began undressing, gratefully shedding the layers of clothing which so confined and repressed our bodies' natural exuberance.

I stripped to my stays and chemise, then wriggled out of my drawers. The hot sun felt deliciously wicked upon my bare bottom, and I almost giggled out loud.

"Will you unlace my stays, Annabella? Then I shall undo yours."

"You intend to swim naked? But what if…?"

"None will see us, Annabella. The girl told us as much, no one ever comes here but the seabirds and the fish!"

The tightness of my stays melted away as Annabella unlaced me, and I drew in deep, luxurious draughts of sea air. Ah! such freedom, such indulgence. Surely Demelza would not begrudge one moment of peace and pleasure….

I splashed bare-legged into the sea, and was delighted to find the water as warm as a lover's caress.

"Hurry, Annabella, I shall not wait!" I called over my shoulder, then cast myself full-length into the next wave and began striking out for the offshore islet.

I am a strong swimmer, but not as strong as Annabella. Her powerful, athletic body cut smoothly and gracefully through the water, swiftly overtaking me and leaving me many yards behind. And I am forced to admit that this was no great tragedy, for it afforded me an opportunity to appreciate the beauty of her nakedness.

As she slid through the water, its glassy translucence overlaid her skin with a sheen of aquamarine blue, making her seem like some wondrous statue, carved from living stone. Her blonde locks, unpinned and flowing free, spread out behind her like a fan of golden seaweed, their brightness scarcely dimmed by the water.

When at last I came to the islet, Annabella was reclining upon the white sand, her breasts rising and falling from exertion. She was supporting herself on her hands, her head flung back so that rivulets of seawater ran from her wet hair into the sand. Her body, too, was still wet from her swim, the droplets drying swiftly in the late-morning sunshine, her nipples sparkling with water drops that made them seem like rosy jewels.

I pushed back my hair with my hand as I walked up the beach. The sand was scorching beneath my bare feet, the sun beating down on my back. But I paid it no heed. My eyes devoured Annabella, her lips parted and her eyelids drooping lazily over her steel-grey eyes. The hunger in me defied all reason, although I strove to suppress it.

At my approach, Annabella opened her eyes and glanced at me with apparent casualness.

"You should not issue challenges if you are not up to meeting them," she said with an ironic smile.

"I don't recall challenging you to anything, Annabella."

I knew the dangerous game she was playing. She was

trying to force me to admit to some trial of strength between us, trying with all her might to draw me into a battle of wills for the sole purpose of overwhelming and possessing me.

"Really, Elizabeth, you are such a poor loser."

"How can I have lost when there was never any contest?"

She put out her hand and seized me by the wrist.

"Ever since you came seeking me, you have been striving in your own pathetic way to get the better of me. Admit that truth to yourself, if not to me."

"What need have you of truth, Annabella?" I replied with more than a hint of sarcasm, shaking free of her grasp. "When you have your own over-active imagination?"

"You will not speak to me like that!" Annabella seethed. "I will not permit it."

"I have told you before; I shall speak to you exactly as I please."

Annabella rose to her feet.

"You will hold your tongue, or I shall teach you to know your place!"

I grew hot with indignation.

"My *place*, Annabella? How dare you presume!"

Annabella's hand seized me by the hair and twisted it, so suddenly that she made me stumble and fall to my knees on the sand.

"Your place, Elizabeth. On your knees before your Mistress."

I glared up at her through a mist of tears, defiantly unshed though the pain Annabella was inflicting upon me was extraordinarily intense.

"You will never be my Mistress," I spat; and, lunging forward, I succeeded in raking my fingernails down Annabella's flank, leaving four parallel scratches beaded with blood.

"Little bitch!" Annabella snarled, flinging herself upon me. Our bodies locked and, kicking and biting, we rolled over and over at the margin of the lapping waves. "I will subdue you!"

"Never," I panted. "Never, do you hear!"

And to my sudden and infinite horror, I only just prevented myself from adding: You will never be my Mistress, Annabella, because, in our hearts, you and I shall only ever know one Mistress.

And she is Claudia Dungarrow.

Istanbul was huge: a great melting-pot of an Eastern city, teeming with life and noise. I had never encountered anything like it in my life, and indeed found myself quite frightened by the constantly pawing hands, the leering faces, the enigmatic eyes behind many-layered veils.

At length, having failed in all our attempts to obtain information, Annabella and I fell to squabbling.

"If it were not for you…"

"I wish I had never set eyes upon you…"

141

"It is entirely your fault…"

"Poor Demelza, because of you she will never be saved…"

It was in the midst of this pointless altercation that I noticed a long file of women, heads bowed, swathed in voluminous cloaks which hid all but the occasional glance of a dark eye and the flash of brightly painted toenails clad in sequined sandals. They were being shepherded by armed soldiers toward a gate in the high stone wall.

"Those women." I pointed them out to Annabella. "Who are they?"

"The women of the Sultan's harem. That is his palace." Her lip curled. "Why? Have you taken a fancy to become one of his concubines? I had not thought that even you were quite such a filthy little slut."

With the greatest difficulty, I succeeded in calming my rising impatience.

"Why do we not seek admittance to the harem? Surely, if anyone would know of Claudia's whereabouts, it would be the women of the royal household. And remember the picture…the imperial eagle…"

Annabella was forced to admit that, although this might not be a desirable solution to our difficulties, it was preferable to our fruitless squabbling. And it proved an easy matter to enter the harem discreetly, by the simple expedient of swathing ourselves in bolts of silken fabric obtained in the city market.

We then presented ourselves at the side gates of the

palace. To our surprise, we were accepted without question as new concubines, and admitted immediately to the harem. As the huge wooden doors were barred behind us, shutting out the outside world, I could not help but wonder if it would be equally easy to get out again. For I had heard terrible stories of harem life, of girls kept prisoner and forced to submit to the insatiable lusts of men….

At the end of many long, cool, high-ceilinged corridors, we encountered gates of gold and turquoise, chained and guarded by two female soldiers: tall, massively built women with bared breasts and wickedly curved swords which swung from belts of silken rope.

"Who seeks to pass?"

"New concubines…for the Sultan's harem."

"You may pass."

The gates were unlocked, and we were admitted to the inner sanctum, the chains jangling as they were fastened behind us. I stood in wonderment for many moments, for the world I had just entered was entirely new to me. The passageway opened out into a huge circular room with a domed ceiling and pillars patterned in blue and gold.

Here and there, gauzy fabrics hung in diaphanous curtains, forming little nooks where women reclined on cushions, sat playing musical instruments, or lay kissing in each other's arms. Through high, latticed windows I caught glimpses of blue sky, but none of the women seemed to hanker after their freedom. On the contrary, I heard nothing but laughter and song, and amiable conversation.

At the very center of the great hall was a sunken pool, filled with pinkish water in which rose and lily petals floated, imparting a wonderfully sensual fragrance. Gone were the all-enveloping draperies which had hidden the women from sight whilst they walked abroad. Two African girls were swimming lazily, lying on their backs so that the chocolate drops of their nipples pointed heavenward, occasionally breaking the surface of the water. The shaven triangles of their sex offered tempting glimpses of dark and pouting lips.

"Whatever shall we do now?" I asked Annabella. For I had not thought much further than gaining entrance to the harem.

Annabella had not much opportunity to respond, for at that moment a petite, chestnut-haired figure rose from one of the piles of cushions and walked across the room toward us. Her breasts were bare, the pierced nipples joined by three fine gold chains. She wore wide-legged pants of diaphanous pink tulle, which enhanced rather than veiled the beauty of slender limbs and a plump, hairless sex. She was a most exotic creature, and yet...there was something curiously familiar about her.

"Welcome," she greeted us in English, with a slight inclination of the head. "You may remove your outer garments, there are no men to see you here, only the women of the harem."

With some reluctance, we obeyed, letting fall the winding cloth which had hidden our Western clothes from sight. Now we were unmasked for what we were: interlopers who might not be met with favour.

The girl's soft brown eyes opened very wide above the veil which concealed the lower half of her face.

"Elizabeth? No, upon my soul it cannot be! Elizabeth Stanbridge—can it really be you?"

As she unhooked the veil to reveal the rest of her face, realization dawned.

"Miranda Tennant!" I clapped my hand to my mouth and turned to Annabella. "It is Miranda Tennant, don't you remember? She and I were both students in Claudia's Natural Sciences class! But Miranda...Miranda, whatever are you doing here, in this...this prison!"

Miranda laughed, and her soft, tinkling laughter was echoed by the other women of the harem, some of whom had drawn closer to satisfy their curiosity about the new arrivals.

"A prison? Oh, my dear Elizabeth, this is very far from being a prison. It is the most liberating place imaginable for a woman of our sensibilities!"

"But why are you here among these sluts and concubines?" Annabella demanded.

Miranda's lips pursed in amusement. "My dear Annabella, I, too, am one of the Sultan's concubines! But before you shrink in horror, let me explain.

"I, too, have become an enthusiast of Doctor Dungarrow's theories of Sapphic devotion. Indeed, so fired was I by her teachings that I determined to live henceforth only among women."

"But what of your parents?" I asked. "What did they think of your resolve?"

"I admit that they were reluctant at first. But then I discovered that by becoming a concubine of the Sultan I could enter a paradise of Sapphic pleasure, without bringing any dishonour upon my family. You see, my dear Elizabeth, I am concubine in name only. The Sultan has so many hundreds of wives and women that he cannot even hope to meet them all, let alone force his favours upon them. Indeed, this part of the harem is set aside for those who wish to live in the purity of sisterly affection. It is a gift to the Sultan's wife."

Miranda laughed. "And of course there was another benefit to the bargain, as far as my father was concerned."

"And what might that be?"

"I fetched an excellent price. The Sultan was obliged to give my father an island in the Gulf of Oman—which I am sure will bring him far greater pleasure than I ever did! Now, my dears, you must eat and drink while you tell me what has brought you here."

Miranda took us to a secluded corner of the harem, and brought us dishes of sticky Arabian sweetmeats with thick Turkish coffee and glasses of cool sherbet.

"We are looking for Claudia," I explained. "We must find her as a matter of urgency."

My heart sank. Even before Miranda shook her head, I could tell that she had no idea where Claudia might be.

"I would know if she were in Istanbul," Miranda assured us. "She has always taken a great deal of... personal interest in the harem. It is a model of the love and pleasure which only women can share."

Suddenly tired and demoralized, I hung my head. "It is hopeless," I sighed. "We shall never find her. Oh poor, poor Demelza!"

Miranda took my hand and carried it to her lips. "Whatever you seek, you will find it."

Annabella made to rise to her feet. "We must find a way to leave this place."

But Miranda took her arm. "No, my dear, you must stay here tonight. It would not be safe for you to leave now. Better to wait until the dark hours just before dawn. I will make sure that you are able to leave in safety."

"You are very kind," I said. And, in truth, I could think of nothing I wanted more than to remain in this soft and gentle place, to sink down on a pile of down-filled velvet pillows and drift off into a dreamless sleep.

"Not at all. But there are certain precautions we must take."

Annabella looked alarmed.

"Precautions?"

"To ensure that you are not discovered when the eunuchs make their evening inspection. There are certain things which would mark you out instantly as strangers."

"What things?"

Miranda smiled.

"Nothing burdensome, dear Annabella. It is simply that your body must be shaved: no woman of the harem wears any body hair. And then we must paint the symbols of ownership upon your flesh—they will easily be washed off later. You must not worry!" She clapped her hands. "Come, sisters, let us prepare our guests; it is not long until dusk."

It was a long time since my body had been shaved; not since Claudia Dungarrow had abducted me and made me her bond slave. And certainly I had never undergone such an intimate procedure in the presence of so many giggling, caressing, beautiful little minxes. Within moments their exploring fingers had stripped me of my gown and shift, and it took scarcely seconds for them to untie my stay-laces and free me from their closeting embrace.

One of the dark-skinned girls pranced round the hall, Annabella's whaleboned stays pressed to her slender waist, laughing fit to burst.

"See, sisters, now I am a fine English lady!"

One of the other girls, a velvet-skinned Chinese, looked on in round-eyed wonderment. "However can you bear to wear such things?"

"They are the custom in England."

"But they are so…confining!"

Miranda explained, "Here no one is permitted to wear any garment which restricts the natural movement and freedom of the body. Except, of course, for the purposes of discipline."

"And how is discipline administered?" Annabella sensed a subject after her own heart.

"By means of devices which have been constructed to compress and over-stimulate certain parts of the body. The experience is most effective and very instructive; few ever need to be punished more than once."

I determined that, if at all possible, I should avoid being punished at all. I had the distinct impression that Miranda's "devices" would more than meet with Claudia Dungarrow's approval.

The Chinese girl, Mae-Li, returned with a porcelain bowl filled to the brim with creamy lather, and two brushes with wooden handles and soft bristles of pure sable.

"Relax, dear Elizabeth," purred Miranda, urging me to lay myself down on the cushions she had arranged carefully. "Draw up your knees and try not to tense yourself. Allow yourself to accept the simple pleasure of the razor's caress."

It took more than a little will to abandon fear and trust to Miranda's skill with the cutthroat razor. Its blade was wickedly sharp and glinted menacingly as she wiped it on a white towel and pressed it lightly against the flesh of my belly, drawing it smoothly down over my pubic bone in a single sweeping movement.

To my surprise, it was exactly as Miranda had described: a pleasure, simple yet curiously intense. And perhaps, if I am honest, the pleasure was all the greater because of the element of danger. For as the blade swept and skated across my skin, revealing the nakedness of my sex, I could not banish from my mind the possibility of sudden sharp pain. A blissful possibility, too shameful to be openly confessed.

And I closed my eyes and let out my breath in a long, shimmering sigh, imagining that the razor's sweep was the rasp of a she-tiger's tongue, moments before the bite of her deadly teeth.

CHAPTER 10

The following morning, a little before dawn, Miranda kissed us a fond farewell and ushered us silently to the side door of the palace, allowing us to slip out unseen into the velvety darkness.

The life of the harem had revealed itself to be surprisingly pleasurable and very restoring to the soul; but alas, our good humor did not last long. When all was said and done, our sojourn in the Sultan's harem had provided us with an agreeable interlude, but nothing more. Even when we were seated on the luxurious Orient Express, heading away from Istanbul and westward toward Italy, Annabella and I scarcely ceased bickering long enough to draw breath.

"Poor Demelza!" Annabella gazed stubbornly out of the window. "We have failed her; it is all up with her now."

"We must not give up!" I protested, thinking of poor Demelza lying in her bed at Annabella's house, sinking ever deeper into a sleep from which she might never recover. "How can you suggest such a monstrous thing?"

"If it were not for me, Elizabeth, neither of us would suggest anything worth considering. You have proved perfectly useless in this matter, as I might have guessed that you would."

"And you would have fared better on your own, I suppose?"

"I could scarcely have fared worse!"

We sat in malevolent silence for a while, punctuated only by the sound of the train wheels rattling over the rails. Then I reached across and picked up Annabella's carpetbag.

"What are you doing? Put that down at once!"

I ignored her with serene contempt, opened the bag and took out the picture which had baffled us for so long.

"You can see what I am doing, Annabella. Do be quiet and let me think."

Annabella's petulant response was to snatch the picture from me and attempt to tear it in two; but I succeeded in rescuing it from her before she did any significant damage. From somewhere—I know not exactly where—I found a hidden reserve of steel.

"Annabella, you are behaving like a spoilt child! Shut up and think. For Demelza's sake, think!"

Annabella's mouth hung open for a moment, like a startled goldfish's, then snapped shut. The color seemed to drain momentarily from her cheeks, then was replaced by a faint blush of humiliation. I do not deny a fleeting rush of exhilaration at having, however briefly, put a stop to her arrogance.

"What is there to think about? We are done for."

"No. No, we are not. Claudia would not have set this riddle for us if we were not capable of solving it. She wants us to solve it, don't you see? If we fail, she will not have the satisfaction of continuing her wicked game."

Annabella conceded that this might, perhaps, be true. And she deigned to move a little closer, the better to inspect the picture.

"One last effort?"

"One. And if we are still defeated, perhaps then we shall give up." Or perhaps not, I told myself. For I would never give up in my attempt to save Demelza— not until my very last breath.

"It is definitely an imperial eagle," Annabella commented. "And a river."

"So the place we seek is an imperial city, built on a river."

"It would seem so. But this letter 'V'—it must have some significance. Could it be the name of a person? An emperor—Vespasian, perhaps?"

153

"Or the capital letter of a city? We have been to Vienna. There is Versailles…Venice…Valencia, Varennes, even Vilnius—the list is endless!"

Annabella shook her head.

"We have only days left, we cannot explore all these places. It is hopeless. That bitch Dungarrow has defeated us."

And then it came to me, in a lightning flash of inspiration which made me wonder at my own stupidity for all these weeks.

"No, Annabella, it is none of those cities. Don't you see?"

Annabella regarded me coldly. "I see nothing but a silly child who cannot even make herself clearly understood."

"It isn't a city, and it certainly isn't the name of an emperor. Claudia would never choose a man. It is our own dear Empress Victoria!"

Annabella stared at me.

"Victoria? The Queen? But…?"

"And the river—it is the River Thames, at Windsor, where the Queen is currently in residence! That bridge in the picture—it must be the bridge that leads from Windsor to Eton!"

This time, every ounce of color drained from Annabella's face, as suddenly and completely as if she were the victim of some vampiric embrace.

"Of course!" she whispered, almost inaudibly. "Eugenia…"

"Annabella? I don't understand."

"Claudia, Claudia you scheming bitch!"

I was genuinely alarmed by the look on Annabella's face. And when I touched her arm, I found that she was shaking all over.

"Annabella, whatever ails you?"

Her grey eyes met mine. Their gaze was steady and cold, but it was not difficult to tell that there was pain behind that studied lack of expression.

"I know now whom we are looking for. It was obvious all the time, only I could not bear to think of it. Claudia Dungarrow has sought out the bitterest pain in my heart, Elizabeth, the one great regret of my life.

"We are looking for my first and only love, the woman who stole away my heart and my maidenhead when I was but eighteen. The woman who tore that heart in two and left it forever bleeding when we were forced apart."

"Who is she, Annabella?" I could scarcely believe that such depth of emotion could exist within coldhearted, stern-faced Annabella Fitzgerald.

"Her name is Princess Eugenia of Montenegro," replied Annabella, her voice a tremulous whisper. "And she is one of Queen Victoria's most trusted ladies-in-waiting."

I am not sure what I expected of Princess Eugenia. In the days between leaving Istanbul and arriving back in

England, I had ample opportunity to imagine her face, her mannerisms, the body which had so captivated Annabella that even now, years later, she could scarcely bear to speak of her.

Obtaining entrance to the Princess's private apartments proved well-nigh impossible, for the Queen was in residence and orders had been given that no members of the public were to be admitted. But Annabella scribbled a message on one of her calling cards and handed it to the sentry, with instructions to see that it was delivered directly to Princess Eugenia. Within five minutes, we were permitted to enter.

A housemaid ushered us up to the first-floor apartments, knocking on the door and announcing our arrival.

"Lady Annabella Fitzgerald and Miss Elizabeth Stanbridge, ma'am."

A voice answered from within, in calm and measured tones. It was a musical voice, rather low in pitch and smooth and soft as velvet. I could well imagine how even Annabella Fitzgerald might be captivated by such a voice.

"Show them in. Then leave and lock the door behind you."

This alarmed me somewhat, but we were in no position to argue. A slight shiver ran down my spine as I heard the key turn in the lock behind us, then silence.

Princess Eugenia of Montenegro was standing at the

window, gazing out over the castle to the bustling world down below. She presented a striking figure, quite tall and seemingly taller because of her very slender frame and high-heeled white boots, visible beneath the frilled hem of her dramatic gown of white silk, trimmed with mauve satin roses. Her glossy brown hair was worn in a high, elaborate style, secured with jewel-headed pins and a sprig of fresh roses.

"Such peasants," she remarked. "They think themselves so important to live in the shadow of the castle, yet they are nothing. Mere ants. They have no conception of the nature of true power."

She swung around to face us, and I saw her full beauty for the first time. Her face was a slender oval, her lips full and naturally deep rose-pink. Her pale skin and long swanlike throat led down to small, high-set breasts set off by a triple collar of diamonds and pearls.

"Annabella." She spoke the word with infinite care, as though experiencing it for the first time, her pale golden eyes denying themselves the weakness of expression. "Your message spoke of life and death."

Annabella took one step forward, but could go no farther.

"I...have come here from necessity. To seek out Claudia Dungarrow. My sister's life depends upon your help."

The Princess nodded slowly. "Yes."

"You know where she is?"

"The picture brought you here, did it not?"

"It did."

"Then you know that I hold the information you seek."

Pain seemed to cross the Princess's face, and I darted a glance at Annabella. She was white-lipped and trembling, clearly exercising a supreme effort of will to hold back the force of her emotions.

"Then you must tell us!" I cried out impetuously. "We must know, for Demelza's sake. You must not hold back the truth from us."

The Princess seemed not to hear me. Her eyes were fixed upon Annabella.

"I owe a great deal to Claudia Dungarrow," she whispered hoarsely, as though the words caused her physical distress. "A debt which will be many years in the repaying. She has instructed me…"

Suddenly the Princess's legs seemed to give way beneath her, and she sank to the floor, convulsed by sobs. Annabella ran to her, lifting her up, cradling her in her arms.

"Eugenia, Eugenia!"

"I cannot.… She commands me, yet I cannot do it!"

Annabella showered Eugenia's face with feverish kisses, and all at once Eugenia was responding, her hands caressing Annabella's hair, her shoulders, her breasts.

"Hush, hush, Eugenia. We shall not speak of it. Come into my arms and let me soothe your pain."

It was a touching scene. Never had I thought Annabella capable of such tenderness as she laid the Princess down upon the Chinese silk carpet and began kissing and caressing her like some fragile and priceless object of undying passion.

Their bodies melted into each other, the Princess's skirts riding up to reveal no underclothing save petticoats and a golden chain, running between her thighs from rings set into love-lips and arse. Annabella's kisses followed the line of the chain hungrily, devouring smooth flesh, gently pushing apart the Princess's thighs and exploring the moistness of her pleasure with lips and tongue and teeth.

"Ah! Ah no, no you mustn't, I must not yield!" gasped the Princess, but her protests were all in vain, for her body had already yielded and her spirit could not long resist the rising tide of desire.

Annabella took the golden chain between her lips and began toying with it as she slipped one finger deep into the Princess's honeypot. This caused the Princess no little distress, and she began writhing and moaning, wetness coursing from her and oozing onto the carpet beneath her backside.

"Oh my princess, my lustful princess, do you remember how we kissed? How we caressed? Do you remember how you took my maidenhead that hot June afternoon, in my uncle's orchard…?"

"Annabella, Annabella…"

The protests were growing fainter now, and it was plain to see that Annabella had the measure of the Princess, judging with expert kisses and caresses how far she could go before turning tyrannical desire into merciful release.

"That afternoon...you were my companion, do you remember how we adored each other? We were such innocent girls. And you awakened the first sweet lusts of womanhood within me. Do you recall how you placed your mouth upon my pussy—exactly so?—and teased my clitty with your tongue while your wicked, beautiful fingers forced their way into the virgin heart of me?"

It was a scene of such passion that I was forced to turn my head. The Princess's cries grew softer and softer, until I heard nothing but a softly shimmering sigh; and turning back, I saw that she and Annabella were kissing passionately, their tears mingling as they held each other tightly.

At last Eugenia broke free of the kiss. "I must not. I must not.... Claudia...her anger..."

Annabella seized her shoulders. "What did she command you to do?"

"To humiliate you, to punish you, to refuse you the information you need until you are utterly broken in spirit. To torment you. But...but I cannot...."

"Where is she, Eugenia? Where is Claudia?"

"At Grantchester. In her own house."

"The Manor!"

"Yes, Annabella. She has been playing games with you. And...And with me." Eugenia got to her feet slowly and uncertainly. "Annabella...I have given you what you wanted; now you must promise me one thing."

"Name it."

"I swore to Claudia that I would make you suffer terrible agony. Please...for my sake, lie to her. Tell her of the great pain you have suffered because of this meeting."

Annabella's hand touched the Princess's briefly, but there was a world of tenderness and regret in the touch.

"I shall not need to lie," she replied softly. "And in your heart you know it. For nothing in the world—no whip, no knife, no betrayal—could have caused me more pain than seeing you again."

No carriage, no train, no wild horse could have carried us swiftly enough across the many miles from Windsor to Grantchester.

We were fortunate in obtaining a train to London that very evening; but in order to continue our journey through the night we were obliged to hire a carriage which moved with frustrating slowness along the rutted country roads.

"Faster, you dolt!" Annabella shouted, but the coachman simply shrugged and drew his head down into the collar of his overcoat.

"Any faster and you'll have us in a ditch, miss," he

grunted, and the horses ambled on through the night. "Everythin' comes to those who wait; that's what my old mother used to say."

"But we have no time to wait," Annabella hissed between clenched teeth, her words lost in the muffling darkness.

Rain was drumming on the roof of the carriage as we drew into the yard of a coaching inn, there to obtain a change of horses. It was pitch-black and a truly filthy night, with wind lashing the rooftops of the little town and turning each flitting shadow into a howling demon.

"A few hours here and we'll be off," said the coachman.

"But we must leave now!" Annabella protested.

"A man must have his sleep an' his ale, miss. An' that's all there is to it."

"But there must be some other way!" I cried.

He shook his head. "Ain't no way of gettin' out of here, missus. Not in the middle of the night, at any rate. So you'd best make the best of it an' get some sleep."

And the coachman promptly took himself off to bed, forcing us to take a room and spend the rest of a sleepless night counting the raindrops as they lashed against the windowpane.

The following day we set off again at last, not in the company of our laconic coachman, but on foot to the nearest railway station, where we managed to obtain seats as far as Cambridge. From there, we would have to manage as best we could.

Every second passed with agonizing slowness, every station-halt twisting my nerves to breaking point. We had but hours left before the end of the month which Claudia had set us to find her. Would we succeed in reaching the Manor before nightfall?

The rain did not let up all day. The ground turned to a muddy swamp, the meadows to green lakes where cows paddled ankle-deep in overflowing river.

"Two hours, Annabella. That is all we have left."

"We shall get there in time, Elizabeth. We must."

And so it was that at Cambridge we hired two of the swiftest horses we could find, mounted up—leaving our luggage at the railway station for safekeeping—and set off at a gallop for Grantchester.

So fierce was the rain that my clothes were stuck to my body, my hair sodden and plastered to my face in dripping tendrils. I could scarcely grip the reins—they were so slippery with rainwater—and it was almost impossible to see where we were going. But I did not need to see the road: the way to Claudia Dungarrow's house is forever engraved upon my soul.

"Faster, Annabella, hurry! There is but half an hour's time left."

And at last, scant minutes before the appointed time, I glimpsed the Manor through the cascading rainwater: the elegant, mysterious, terrifying place of my sexual awakening and my enslavement. For a brief second, I thought of reining in my horse, wheeling him round and galloping away, with never a backward look. To go forward was to walk with open eyes into Claudia's trap, like a fly throwing itself wantonly onto a spider's web.

But turning back would betray my darling Demelza, and that I could never do. My mind was already made up. I spurred on the horse and galloped up to the front steps of the Manor.

Hammering on the door, we waited for an agonizing eternity, the entire world filled with the monotonous, ominous drumming of the rain upon the ground. At last the door swung open.

The Indian servant greeted us. She was young and very beautiful, just as I remembered her, only this time, Indhira was naked save for a delicate skein of golden chains which hung from piercings in her nipples, lips, and navel.

"Welcome." She pressed her palms together and bowed her head respectfully. "Please enter. The Mistress is expecting you."

From the journal of Claudia Dungarrow:
Dear, sweet Demelza. She is so tractable. Everything a darling slut ought to be—which is perhaps why I find Elizabeth and Annabella so much more stimulating.

And why I had determined to overcome them both. For their willful spirits could never be truly at peace except in the brooding shadow of my dark love.

"Mistress." The ecstatic whisper escaped unbidden from Demelza's lips.

"Hush, sweet slut. You must keep your pleasure silent until you are bidden to speak."

"Forgive me," she murmured sleepily, lost in a many-colored dreamworld of unending pleasure. "Forgive me...beloved Mistress...."

Dear child. So obedient and so contrite. And so ethereally beautiful, her pale-gold hair spread out about her elfin face and her slender white limbs stretched out across the frame of the grand piano. Her flesh was taut and tense, her ribs visible beneath the pale skin and her breasts contracted to small, roundels of plumpness, cherry-tipped and inviting.

Demelza's sensual peony-red mouth blossomed into a beatific smile as I wound the wire round and round her body, twisting it about her limbs, tightening it, binding her ever more closely to the open pianoforte. From between her outspread thighs crept sweet, viscous drops of honeydew, forming trembling tears on the piano strings. I struck a key, and the note seemed to vibrate through her, striking some echoing harmony within her lustful frame. And then another, low and mellifluous, setting the strings beneath her backside quivering with sonorous harmony.

"Ah. Ah, yes, yeees...."

Dear slut. So easily satisfied, so completely loyal to your only Mistress. Not like your headstrong sister, or that rebellious wench Elizabeth, with her hellcat eyes and fury-spitting lips. Such sluts must be taught obedience, taught it again and again until they become incapable of understanding anything else.

I ran my fingers lightly down Demelza's thigh, feeling the faint hardness of muscle beneath the soft flesh. My fingers walked a little higher, provoking quiet moans of excitation as Demelza anticipated still-greater pleasures. Pleasures which I would most likely have accorded her—for she had pleased me and it is my habit to reward obedient behavior—but at that moment Indhira knocked and entered the room.

I turned stony eyes upon her. "How dare you interrupt me, slut!"

Indhira bobbed a curtsy, making all her golden chains jingle and glitter in the evening sunlight.

"May it please you, madam, the two English ladies..."

My fist clenched in triumphant joy, jerking hard upon the wires which bound my dear Demelza to her rack of blissful pain.

"They are here? Miss Stanbridge and Lady Annabella?"

"Yes, madam. They are waiting in—"

But of course, they were not waiting. Bidden by Indhira to remain in the hallway, they had naturally disregarded her instructions and followed her like wild dogs. The door burst open with furious haste, and in tumbled Elizabeth and Annabella, soaked to the skin and shivering in their wet clothes.

"Bitch!" Annabella screeched. "Bitch from Hell!"

Elizabeth's eyes widened in horror as she saw Demelza, spread-eagled across the piano.

"Oh, Demelza, my dear one! My sweet, what terrible thing has been done to you?"

I did not answer their impetuous rantings, but simply smiled and extended the hand of sweet friendship.

"My dear sluts. Welcome to the Hall. Welcome at last."

CHAPTER 11

From the journal of Elizabeth Stanbridge:
I could scarcely believe it. Poor darling Demelza, naked and cruelly bound by sharp wires to a piano frame, whilst Claudia Dungarrow stood by, smiling with an evil serenity which chilled my blood.

I sprang forward, but Annabella had already anticipated my thoughts.

"Bitch, harpy, harridan—I swear I will destroy you for what you have done to my sister!"

She flew like a screaming wildcat at Claudia, claws outstretched, a spitting fury, her hair turned to tangled serpents that would have done credit to the head of Medusa. But, to my astonishment—and evidently Annabella's also—Claudia made no attempt to resist. On the contrary, she stood perfectly still, allowing Annabella to pull her wrists behind her back and hold them fast.

"Elizabeth," Annabella gasped. "Quickly—untie Demelza!"

I needed no further bidding, though astonishment and doubt made me cast glances over my shoulder at Claudia's enigmatic smile. With cold and fumbling fingers I pulled and tore at the wire, releasing Demelza little by little, until her nakedness was in my arms, her white skin blemished with a crisscross pattern of red lines where the wires had dug into it.

"Demelza," I sobbed, embracing her and helping her to her feet. "Demelza, you shall never be so cruelly treated again. I swear it!"

But a coldness gripped my heart as I looked into Demelza's eyes. She was staring ahead of her blankly, apparently neither seeing nor recognizing me.

"She does not know me!" I cried out.

Annabella flung Claudia hard against the side of the piano. Claudia made not the slightest effort to free herself or retaliate, and that frightened me almost more than poor Demelza's trance-like state.

"What have you done to her?" Annabella snarled, striking Claudia across the cheek. Claudia's smile did not flicker for an instant; if anything, it merely became more smug.

"She cannot see you," Claudia said quietly. "But she

responds beautifully to my commands. Isn't that right, my sweet one?"

At this, Demelza turned her head toward Claudia.

"Yes, Mistress," she whispered, her voice hushed and respectful.

"You would do anything for me, wouldn't you, Demelza?"

"Anything...Mistress."

"What does this mean?" I cried, taking Demelza by the shoulders and shaking her, hoping that by physical force I might bring her back to her senses. But her spirit retreated from me, sunk deep in some hypnotic trance which only Claudia could penetrate.

"Die for me, Demelza."

"Mistress?"

"Die for me. Now."

To my horror, Demelza pushed me away, with such unexpected force that I stumbled back and let go of her. With her right arm she stretched out and snatched a knife from the wall; a fearsome Gurkha weapon with a wickedly sharp, curving blade.

"No, Demelza, no!" Annabella shouted. But if Demelza heard her sister, she paid her no heed. She lifted the knife with both hands and pressed its tip between her breasts.

"Stop her, Claudia! Stop her!"

"I do not take orders from sluts, Elizabeth. Particularly disobedient sluts like you. And the only commands Demelza heeds come from me."

My head swam. I froze in terror, unable to move. Annabella's eyes were wide with fear. It seemed that in a moment's time, Demelza would end her life, and there was nothing we could do to prevent her.

And then Claudia spoke again. Shaking free of Annabella's weakened grip, she clapped her hands.

"Demelza—wait!" The knife tumbled from Demelza's hands, falling softly to the carpeted floor.

"Mistress?"

Claudia clapped her hands a second time.

"You may wake now."

Demelza blinked, swayed and put out a hand to steady herself. I caught her in my arms. Claudia looked from Annabella to me and back again, and her smile grew more serene.

"Now, my dear sluts, won't you join us for dinner?"

What could we do but accept Claudia's "invitation," though we abhorred the very ground upon which she stood? And what could we do but accept her offer of clean, dry clothes, since our own were soaked and half-ruined by rainwater and mud?

And yet, dear reader, you can imagine what feelings entered my breast as Indhira led me up the stairs to Claudia's private bathroom and showed me the clothes which I was to wear: the selfsame dress of white muslin, trimmed with yellow satin rosebuds, which she gave me to wear on the day she first seduced my honor!

At last we descended to the dining hall, I nervous and self-conscious in my yellow-and-white décolleté, Annabella statuesque in a close-fitting gown of wine-red satin.

Claudia greeted us cordially. She was standing at the head of the table, very sleek and feline in an extraordinary confection of black leather: the bodice loosely laced to reveal the inner swell of her full breasts, the skirt slashed so that it fell like the petals of some unholy flower, stirring when she walked to provide tantalizing glimpses of shiny red boots and gartered black stockings.

"Ah, dear sluts. Enter. Refresh yourselves." She snapped her fingers and Demelza approached, to my dismay naked save for a small frilled apron and crawling like a kitten on hands and knees. "Bring our guests a glass of champagne."

"At once, Mistress."

I watched, sickened yet curiously excited, as Demelza smothered her Mistress's boots with kisses.

"You may rise."

"Thank you Mistress."

She walked to the sideboard and poured three glasses of champagne, presenting the tray first to Claudia.

"Foolish girl. You must serve our guests first."

"Forgive me, Mistress Claudia."

I hesitated before taking a glass from the tray, exchanging looks with Annabella. Could we trust anything we might consume in this place? The very air of the Hall seemed thick with incense and strange Oriental perfumes which made the senses swim.

"Will you not accept a glass, my dear Elizabeth?" Demelza spoke the words so prettily that I at once took a glass and sipped from it. Her full carmined lips curved into a radiant smile. "Oh, thank you. Thank you, my dear Elizabeth."

The same pantomime was repeated with Annabella. Strange feelings stirred in my belly as I watched Demelza going about her duties. She played the little bond slave to perfection, never setting a foot wrong, never showing the slightest sign of defiance.

Claudia saw me watching her and smiled. "I have trained her well, don't you agree?"

"You have broken her spirit and destroyed her!" Annabella snapped back. "And for that sin I can never forgive you."

Claudia sighed like an indulgent parent whose patience has been tried once too often.

"Dear Annabella. Still so pious and unyielding. I see that I still have a great deal to teach you."

"I do not intend giving you the opportunity to teach me anything!"

"Well, we shall have to see about that, shan't we? First, let us enjoy our dinner. I trust you like Indian food?"

Claudia snapped her fingers. Demelza sprang to her side.

"Mistress?"

"You may serve the first course."

"At once, Mistress."

With more kisses and curtsies, Demelza disappeared from the dining room.

"A good slut," commented Claudia. "Obedient and willing. Not like some…"

"I am not your slut, Claudia," I retorted defiantly. "Not now, not ever."

Claudia did not rise to the bait. She simply went on smiling, patronizing and smug.

"So you have ceased to find me…fascinating, Elizabeth?"

I felt my cheeks burn. Even after so many months' separation, Claudia seemed to have the power to read deep into my soul.

"I was never fascinated by you," I lied. "Not in the least."

"Why don't you try the *chana dhal* and chicken shashlik? Indhira has prepared them specially." Claudia placed a definite emphasis on the word "specially." For a moment, I wondered whether she had put something into the food—perhaps the same strange hypnotic drug with which she had gained possession of poor Demelza's soul. "I can assure you, Elizabeth, there is not the slightest danger."

For some reason, I know not why, I threw caution to the winds and began eating. Certainly the food was exquisite, a blend of Eastern spices I had never tasted before. And Annabella seemed to be eating, too, so what danger could there be? If carried to excess, suspicion could become less a justifiable emotion than a contemptible habit.

My head was spinning a little, but I put that down to the champagne. I am not accustomed to drinking much alcohol, and champagne is such a dizzy, frivolous drink that it never fails to go to my head. I put my hand to my temple and tried to shake away the confusion, but my next sip of champagne only succeeded in adding to the treacherous warmth which was creeping down into my belly.

"Is something wrong, Elizabeth?" Claudia inquired with apparent concern.

"N-No. Nothing."

"It is very...warm in here," Annabella remarked, her face rather flushed despite the coolness of the evening. I could not help noticing that her pupils were greatly dilated, just as Demelza's had been when she fell into her trance....

"You think so?" Claudia's fingers played with the twisted stem of her glass. "Perhaps you should loosen the bodice of your gown."

"Why have you brought us here?" demanded Annabella, who seemed to be having difficulty in focusing. "What evil game is this? Have you brought us here only to humiliate us?"

176

"Game, my dear sluts? Surely you know me well enough to understand that everything I do is in deadly earnest." Claudia considered for a moment. "It seems I overestimated your combined intellect, which is rather a pity. It took you a very great deal of time to find me—still, I suppose you did your best."

"How dare you taunt us!" I exclaimed, trying to rise from my seat but finding it unaccountably difficult. Such a sensual warmth had entered my soul that I could scarcely think of anything else. My mind seemed inexplicably clouded, filled with fleeting images which disturbed and seduced: Demelza on her knees, displaying the ruby fruit of her sex; Annabella's tongue disappearing into the long, moist tunnel: Claudia with one foot on the seat of her chair, parting her skirts to reveal the pierced flesh of her shaven pussy….

"Calm yourself, Elizabeth," Claudia purred. "All shall be well—isn't that so, Demelza?"

Demelza, who was kneeling at her mistress's feet, raised her eyes and smiled. "Oh, yes, Mistress. All has been bliss since you brought me here and made me your slave. Never have I known such happiness as I have known in your service."

"It cannot be!" Annabella exclaimed. "You ask me to believe that you are happy here? Demelza, come to me, look into my eyes and swear that this is true."

"Gladly, sister." Demelza looked to her Mistress for permission.

Claudia nodded. "By all means go to them. Reassure them. Prove to them that your Mistress Claudia Dungarrow has brought you nothing but the most intense pleasure."

Demelza got to her feet and walked round the table, very slowly, until she was standing in front of Annabella.

"Sister, oh, sister, you must not be angry with me. Say you are not angry."

She took Annabella's hands in hers.

"Of course I am not angry, Demelza, but—"

"Hush, sister." Standing on tiptoe, Demelza pressed her crimson-painted mouth against her sister's. "Let this kiss signify the love between us, sister."

She turned to me, her mouth moist and oh so very red, as though she had sipped fresh blood and not thought to lick it from her lips. Momentarily afraid, I took a step backward, but Demelza kept on coming toward me.

"Elizabeth, my dear one. My sweet. Let us kiss and be friends and lovers forever."

Her kiss thrilled me in a way I cannot explain, even now. But as her lips met mine, a most extraordinary sensation thrilled through me: a feeling of intense cold and heat mingled; and shivering, quivering, irrepressible desire bubbled up within me as though from some subterranean spring.

"Demelza—no!" Too late I pushed her from me, realizing the stratagem with which Claudia had tricked us.

The carmine paint on Demelza's lips—it must contain some narcotic substance, some devilish Eastern concoction....

But realization came much, much too late. Already the warmth within me was turning to a raging furnace of desire. My body began to twist and turn instinctively in an agony of lust, helpless to escape the needs which grew with each passing second.

Hopelessly enthralled by desire, I looked at Annabella, and knew that it was happening to her, too. Her eyes were wide; her breathing was fast and shallow; her fingers clawed her bodice.

"Poor dear sluts," Claudia purred. Her voice sounded curiously distant, and everything I looked at seemed blurred and unnaturally bright, the colors so magnified that they were almost unbearably intense. I closed my eyes, but my torment only increased. I imagined tongues and fingers exploring my body, nails clawing my flesh, a smoothly polished double-headed dildo ramming deep into the willing heart of me, making me a twofold prisoner of my desire.

And, more terrible still, when I opened my eyes again, I discovered that I had imagined nothing. Demelza was on her knees before me, lifting up my skirt and kissing my sex; Annabella's hands sliding up the backs of my thighs, to cup the bare globes of my buttocks and ease them apart.

As I shuddered with guilty pleasure, I stood rooted to

the spot, no more able to escape than if I had been steeped in ether and impaled like a butterfly in a glass case. My brain was shrieking: *You must escape! You must resist!* But my limbs refused to obey my commands, and even my cries turned to dust in my throat. With every second I was sinking deeper, dragged down into a whirlpool of wild sensations. Never in my life had I felt anything so intense, so seductive, so irresistible.

Claudia released a button at her waist, and the skirt of her gown slithered to the ground in a swish of black leather. She stepped out of it, moving toward me with long, deliberate strides, her red boots and black silk stockings throwing into relief the shaven whiteness of her sex, pierced not once but by a dozen jingling golden rings.

She took my chin in her hands and forced my mouth against hers.

"Dear little slut," she murmured. "I knew you would come home to me at last."

I swear that I tried to cry out, to protest, to wrest myself free of her embrace; but desire was far stronger than my resolve, and in my heart I knew that I was lost. I was becoming a prisoner of my own need for pleasure.

And Claudia Dungarrow was turning the golden key.

CHAPTER 12

From the journal of Elizabeth Stanbridge:
I awoke slowly and languidly, sleepily twisting and turning upon the soft feather mattress as pleasure seeped into my consciousness.

A voice whispered to me, sultry and low-pitched.

"How long have you denied yourself pleasure, Elizabeth? Oh, my darling slut, how could you deny your true self for so long?"

My eyes flickered open, blinking in the mellow golden sunlight which was filtering into the room. I started, finding myself quite alone although the voice had seemed very close. And not any voice—the voice of Claudia Dungarrow.

"Do not alarm yourself, Elizabeth. I am not far away. Soon we shall be together again for all eternity, but first you must complete your sensual education."

I sat up slowly, trying to make sense of what was happening. I had no conception of time having passed, but supposed that I must have slept for several hours, for darkness had passed and it was now broad daylight.

The previous night had blurred into a wickedly delicious dream, and I could scarcely distinguish between truth and fantasy. Yet my head was already clearing, and something deep in my soul told me that whatever Eastern potions Claudia had employed upon me to break down my resistance, the effect which they had had upon me was far more than transient.

"Do you recognize where you are, sweet slut?" Claudia's voice inquired. I looked around me, but could not focus upon its source, though I knew she must be spying upon me from one of the peepholes in the wooden wainscoting. An unearthly feeling, part fear and part pleasure, crept over me as I took in my surroundings.

"The Salon..." I murmured softly.

"Yes, dear slut, you are in the very training room I built especially for your seduction. Is it exactly as you remember it?"

She knew that it was. The roughly circular chamber had not changed one whit since I had last seen it, so many long months ago. Instead of windows, it possessed a high-domed, many-colored skylight of painted glass, denying all sight of the outside world. A grand piano, a flute, great quantities of books and erotic etchings—these were the very amusements which Claudia had supplied for my education and initiation into the ways of her service.

Ah yes, the Salon was a magnificent and luxurious prison, in which innocence might be seduced with the perfect ease and precision demanded by Claudia Dungarrow.

A frisson of recollected pain and pleasure made my hand quiver as I stretched it out and smoothed my fingers over the polished walnut of the piano lid. Remembering...

"Exactly the same."

"I am so very glad." There was a satisfied smile in Claudia's voice. "I would not wish to disappoint you, and I am most concerned to ensure that you feel completely at home."

A thought entered my clearing head and I whirled around, facing the imagined source of the voice.

"Demelza...Annabella... Where are they? What have you done with them?" I cried out.

Claudia laughed. "Dear child, still so altruistic—and so eager to rejoin your lovers. Have patience, Elizabeth; they, too, have lessons to learn. The more quickly you learn, the more quickly you shall share pleasure with them again."

Something very curious had happened to me, dear reader, for instead of crying out and beating my fists against the panelling, cursing Claudia and all her works, I found that my soul had been invaded by a kind of dreamy serenity.

"What is it that you wish me to do?"

"Good girl," Claudia purred. "I knew you would see reason. At heart you are not a rebellious slut. Undress yourself, then take a bath: it has been prepared for you. Then go to the armoire and put on the clothes I have prepared for you."

I did as she directed, all thoughts of defiance strangely absent from my mind. As I slipped into the sunken bath, and felt the scented oils caress my bare skin, I knew that the lure of pleasure which Claudia held out to me was proving unaccountably more powerful than any dream of freedom. I ran my hands over my body, meaning to soap myself, but Claudia's voice rang out with sudden sternness.

"No. Do not touch yourself or look at yourself. Not yet. I forbid it. Now step out of the bath and go to the armoire."

The clothing which Claudia had prepared for me was perfectly clear and simple in its symbolism. It consisted of a heavy collar of white leather, studded with silver and attached to a mesh of thick chains which formed a clinking veil over my back and breasts, and were joined to a white leather belt which buckled tightly about my waist. From the waist down, I was evidently to go naked, save for white sandals laced with leather thongs, Roman-style, to a point just above the knee.

"How delightful you look," remarked Claudia. "Draw up the piano stool so that it is in front of the cheval mirror."

I did so.

"And now?"

"Go directly to the toy cupboard and take out what you find there."

Inside the cupboard was a silver box about two feet square, inscribed with Eastern symbols which I could not decipher. I lifted it out and set it on a low table.

"Now open it, Elizabeth. Do it swiftly; do not try my patience."

The lid of the box swung open to reveal a treasury of sexual playthings: nipple clamps in the form of tigers' heads, the spring-loaded jaws powerful and cruelly serrated to resemble teeth; a plug of carved ivory, quite short but the thickness of a woman's wrist; and a massive dildo of polished sandalwood, at least eighteen inches long and three in diameter, ornamented with silver filigree banding at its root.

"Beautiful, are they not? I had them made especially for you, Elizabeth, knowing how they would please you. You see, sweet slut, no one but your Mistress Claudia truly understands your pleasure. Not even yourself."

I closed my eyes for a moment. My fingers explored

the trinkets wonderingly, skating lightly over the aromatic wood, the sharp metal teeth. I breathed in the scents of sandalwood and sex. And a faint echo escaped from between my lips, instinctive and unbidden.

"M-Mistress. Mistress Claudia."

"That's right, Elizabeth. I am pleased to see you relearning obedience so swiftly. Let us ensure that this time you never forget your lessons."

"I...will try, Mistress."

"Take the toys and go to the stool. Sit down. Spread your legs—that's right, very wide. Now, sweet slut, tell me what you see."

I gazed at myself in the mirror, suddenly stricken with a kind of terrified enchantment. Was this unearthly creature really myself, Elizabeth Stanbridge, the respectable governess, accepted in the best society?

I saw a slave in chains, a beautiful green-eyed bond slave; my chestnut hair tousled and tumbling down over a white throat and bare shoulders held in a tightly chained embrace. My eyes moved slowly down, taking in the insolently pert strawberries of my nipples, peeping out from between the mesh of chains; my small waist, cinched tight by the thick leather belt, and my hips, flaring wide as though they sensed the shameless beauty of my exposed sex.

"I...I see..."

I could not say it. My eyes simply kept on staring, at the diamond stud which had been passed neatly though the head of my clitoris, and which was now causing me inescapable sensations of illicit pleasure. How could I not have noticed it before?

"You were pierced when you became my slut, Elizabeth, and now you are my slut again. It seemed only fitting to give you back the badge of your office. Touch it, Elizabeth. Touch it and tell me how it feels."

My fingers crept to the moist, gently pulsating heart of my womanhood, sliding easily towards my clitoris on a fine film of honeydew. I moaned and a tear escaped from my half-closed lids as I touched—very, very lightly—the erect stalk of my desire.

"It—It is more than I can bear."

"All things can be borne, Elizabeth. Take the clamps and put them on."

I hesitated.

"You must do everything I command, Elizabeth."

And, as though directed by some unseen force, my hands moved up to my breasts, snapping the clamps about my nipples. I gasped and fell forward, but still Claudia's voice was urging me on.

"And now the plug, Elizabeth. You know where it goes—don't you, sweet slut?"

"N-No...I can't...I won't..."

"You will, dear child. You know you will, there can be no question of disobedience."

I watched myself in the mirror as my fingers curled about the ivory plug and reached round behind my back, seeking out the secret mouth which pouted in shameful eagerness.

"Quickly, now. You would not wish to displease me."

And indeed I would not. Besides, my self-deflowerment was gaining its own momentum. I was no longer the protagonist, but merely the object; my own hands no longer belonging to me but simply the agents of a superior power. My Mistress's power.

I did not make a sound as the plug slipped smoothly between my buttocks. I knew that crying out would show a reprehensible weakness, and my whole being ached for a chance to win Claudia's favor.

"And now, dear slut, the dildo. Fuck yourself. Watch yourself fucking. And remember that it is your Mistress who has made you what you are."

What I was? I scarcely knew what that might be. But as the giant dildo forced its way into my gaping sex, I understood one truth at least: that Elizabeth Stanbridge had finally come home.

From the journal of Claudia Dungarrow:

My three dear sluts learned their lessons with passable swiftness. Demelza is, of course, of a naturally docile disposition and was already half-trained. But Annabella and Elizabeth supplied me with more than a little amusement before I judged them ready to enter my service and be admitted to the truth of their new situation.

Annabella Fitzgerald's hard-won loyalty I count as a great prize. But it gave me more pleasure than anything to welcome back my darling, errant slut Elizabeth. No wench has more spirit or more aptitude for the sensual arts, and none has ever given me more pleasure.

On the day of their initiation, I unlocked the doors of the adjoining rooms in which Elizabeth and Annabella had been kept prisoner during the completion of their sensual instruction. Looking them up and down, I beckoned to them to step out into the passageway. With delightful submissiveness, they set about kissing my hands and feet, to such excess that I was forced to reprimand them for their ardor.

"You shall do only as you are commanded," I scolded them. "You shall not display affection unless given permission to do so."

"Forgive me, Mistress," Elizabeth whispered. And Annabella hung her head in shame.

Their expressions changed to amazement when I led them out of the house and into the gardens.

"But"—Annabella gazed about her in an uncomprehending stupor—"But this—"

"This is not the Manor!" Elizabeth gasped. "The house is so very alike, and yet these gardens, these hills—"

I silenced them with a wave of my hand.

"My dear, darling, stupid sluts," I sighed indulgently, waving Demelza forward. "Slut, you may apprise your sisters of our new situation."

Demelza smiled like a kitten licking cream from her whiskers. "Sisters," she began, "first of all, we are no longer at the Manor. In fact, we are not in England at all!"

Elizabeth and Annabella stared at each other.

"Not in England? How can that be?" Annabella demanded. "We came to the Manor to rescue Demelza—"

"—and after the evening's entertainment," I cut in dryly, "you fell into a very deep sleep. During which time, I took the precaution of removing my entire household to northern India."

Elizabeth's face turned ashen.

"India? But how…?"

"When you awoke, it was not the next day as you thought, but several weeks later," explained Demelza. "It was the effect of the Eastern aphrodisiacs upon your delicate constitutions. You were unused to such powerful decoctions."

"But we awoke in the Manor!"

I shook my head, beginning to weary of such damnable stupidity.

"You awoke in a perfect replica of the Manor, which I have had constructed just outside the Indian hill-station of Simla. It was perfectly apparent to me that our household could not continue living in England, bearing in mind certain legal matters still outstanding."

Legal matters, I thought to myself, including the theft of almost one million pounds sterling and the attendant police investigations—which might prove awkward were I to attempt to reside permanently in England. Still, the knowledge I have gained of Eastern pharmacy whilst living in India has proved extraordinarily useful to me in my life of amateur crime, and I am confident that our little household shall never again be troubled by a shortage of funds.

"India!" Elizabeth gasped, her green eyes wide as she stood on the neatly manicured lawns and surveyed the rolling hills beyond the town. "But it is so like England, I can scarcely believe it!"

"You shall come to believe it," I reassured her, stroking the long, smooth mass of her hair. "And with your loyal service we shall build a Sapphic empire in these green hills."

"There are others here, Mistress? Others of our persuasion?"

I smiled.

"There are many beautiful young women here, the bored daughters and wives of Indian Army officers. Some have already embraced the Sapphic way; others are still waiting for their eyes to be opened. There is a great deal of important work to do, banishing ignorance and instilling sensual truth.

"You, my darling sluts, will assist me in this work."

And especially you, my dear Elizabeth, I told myself as I pushed her to her knees before me on the grass.

"But before we begin, dear slut, you may lick me out. One can never have sufficient practice in the giving of pleasure."

191

From the journal of Elizabeth Stanbridge:
It is almost a month since Mistress Claudia revealed that we are now living in India. At first, I hardly knew how I would bear being parted from the country of my birth; but in these few short weeks, I have learned to adore Simla and its many sensual possibilities.

Claudia has initiated a program of education for the ladies of Simla, while working on her new philosophical treatise, *Dominance and Submission: Aspects of Sapphic Love.* Besides Claudia's dark beauty, the ladies are much taken with her evident scholarship and authoritative bearing. They flock daily to the afternoon lectures and intimate soirees of her "Sapphic Circle." She lectures them upon the values of discipline and obedience, and Elizabeth, Demelza, and I are constantly on hand to demonstrate the veracity of her statements.

Among the young and the beautiful who attend are certain favorites, young girls who have shown exceptional enthusiasm and promise, and who have already sampled the delights of Mistress Claudia's lessons in submission. Perhaps principal among these is Maddie, a brown-eyed, ash-blonde minx with long, slender limbs and tiny pale breasts whose hard nipples push invitingly against the inside of her flimsy muslin blouse.

My dreams have often been filled with tormenting imaginings, in which Maddie's body becomes the instrument with which I satisfy my every dark desire.

And with each day that passes, I find it more difficult to separate dreams and reality.

This afternoon, while Mistress Claudia was demonstrating the techniques of corporal punishment to her awestruck audience, I made an excuse to slip away and—quite by chance, of course—happened upon dear Maddie as she was walking past the summer-house, half-hidden beside the woodland path.

"You are late for the lecture, Madeleine."

She blushed as I laid my hand upon her shoulder, and hung her head.

"Y-Yes."

I slid my fingers up her throat and over the peach-soft skin of her cheek.

"Address me properly. Say, 'Yes, Mistress.'"

A radiant smile lit up her face and she raised her lips to mine in an ardent kiss. When I released her from my embrace, she was still smiling.

"Yes, Mistress."

"Good girl—you have potential. I can see that from now on, I must take a special interest in your education."

And taking her hand, I led her into the summer-house, secluded from all prying eyes.

Dear reader, pray do not be shocked. It was Mistress Claudia herself who taught me the great truth: that there can be no equality in the relationships between women, one can only dominate or submit. And naturally there can only be one dominatrix. All others must simply be taught submission.

And I, dear reader, am no longer willing to submit.

MASQUERADE BOOKS

MASQUERADE

GERALD GREY
LONDON GIRLS
$6.50/531-X
In 1875, Samuel Brown arrived in London, determined to take the glorious city by storm. And sure enough, Samuel quickly distinguishes himself as one of the city's most notorious rakehells. Young Mr. Brown knows well the many ways of making a lady weak at the knees—and uses them not only to his delight, but to his enormous profit! A rollicking tale of cosmopolitan lust.

OLIVIA M. RAVENSWORTH
THE DESIRES OF REBECCA
$6.50/532-8
A swashbuckling tale of lesbian desire in Merrie Olde England. Beautiful Rebecca follows her passions from the simple love of the girl next door to the relentless lechery of London's most notorious brothel, hoping for the ultimate thrill. Finally, she casts her lot with a crew of sapphic buccaneers, each of whom is more than capable of matching Rebecca lust for lust....

ATAULLAH MARDAAN
KAMA HOURI/DEVA DASI
$7.95/512-3
"...memorable for the author's ability to evoke India present and past.... Mardaan excels in crowding her pages with the sights and smells of India, and her erotic descriptions are convincingly realistic." —Michael Perkins,
The Secret Record: Modern Erotic Literature
Two legendary tales of the East in one spectacular volume. *Kama Houri* details the life of a sheltered Western woman who finds herself living within the confines of a harem—where she discovers herself thrilled with the extent of her servitude. *Deva Dasi* is a tale dedicated to the cult of the Dasis—the sacred women of India who devoted their lives to the fulfillment of the senses—while revealing the sexual rites of Shiva. A special double volume.

J. P. KANSAS
ANDREA AT THE CENTER
$6.50/498-4
Kidnapped! Lithe and lovely young Andrea is whisked away to a distant retreat. Gradually, she is introduced to the ways of the Center, and soon becomes quite friendly with its other inhabitants—all of whom are learning to abandon restraint in their pursuit of the deepest sexual satisfaction. Soon, Andrea takes her place as one of the Center's greatest success stories—a submissive seductress who answers to any and all! A nationally bestselling title, and one of modern erotica's true classics.

VISCOUNT LADYWOOD
GYNECOCRACY
$9.95/511-5
An infamous story of female domination returns to print in one huge, completely unexpurgated volume. Julian, whose parents feel he shows just a bit too much spunk, is sent to a very special private school, in hopes that he will learn to discipline his wayward soul. Once there, Julian discovers that his program of study has been devised by the deliciously stern Mademoiselle de Chambonnard. In no time, Julian is learning the many ways of pleasure and pain—under the firm hand of this beautifully demanding headmistress.

CHARLOTTE ROSE, EDITOR
THE 50 BEST PLAYGIRL FANTASIES
$6.50/460-7
A steamy selection of women's fantasies straight from the pages of *Playgirl*—the leading magazine of sexy entertainment for women. These tales of seduction—specially selected by no less an authority than Charlotte Rose, author of such bestselling women's erotica as *Women at Work* and *The Doctor is In*—are sure to set your pulse racing. From the innocent to the insatiable, these women let no fantasy go unexplored.

N. T. MORLEY
THE PARLOR
$6.50/496-8
Lovely Kathryn gives in to the ultimate temptation. The mysterious John and Sarah ask her to be their slave—an idea that turns Kathryn on so much that she can't refuse! But who are these two mysterious strangers? Little by little, Kathryn not only learns to serve, but comes to know the inner secrets of her stunning keepers.

J. A. GUERRA, EDITOR
COME QUICKLY:
For Couples on the Go
$6.50/461-5
The increasing pace of daily life is no reason to forgo a little carnal pleasure whenever the mood strikes. Here are over sixty of the hottest fantasies around—all designed to get you going in less time than it takes to dial 976. A super-hot volume especially for modern couples on a hectic schedule.

ERICA BRONTE
LUST, INC.
$6.50/467-4
Lust, Inc. explores the extremes of passion that lurk beneath even the coldest, most businesslike exteriors. Join in the sexy escapades of a group of high-powered professionals whose idea of office decorum is like nothing you've ever encountered! Business attire is decidedly not required for this look at high-powered sexual negotiations!

MASQUERADE BOOKS

VANESSA DURIÈS
THE TIES THAT BIND
$6.50/510-7
The incredible confessions of a thrillingly unconventional woman. From the first page, this chronicle of dominance and submission will keep you gasping with its vivid depictions of sensual abandon. At the hand of Masters Georges, Patrick, Pierre and others, this submissive seductress experiences pleasures she never knew existed....

M. S. VALENTINE
THE CAPTIVITY OF CELIA
$6.50/453-4
Colin is considered the prime suspect in a murder, forcing him to seek refuge with his cousin, Sir Jason Hardwicke. In exchange for Colin's safety, Jason demands Celia's unquestioning submission....Sexual extortion!

AMANDA WARE
BINDING CONTRACT
$6.50/491-7
Louise was responsible for bringing many prestigious clients into Claremont's salon—so he was more than willing to have her miss a little work in order to pleasure one of his most important customers. But Eleanor Cavendish had her mind set on something more rigorous than a simple wash and set. Sexual slavery!
BOUND TO THE PAST
$6.50/452-6
Anne accepts a research assignment in a Tudor mansion. Upon arriving, she finds herself aroused by James, a descendant of the mansion's owners. Together they uncover the perverse desires of the mansion's long-dead master—desires that bind Anne inexorably to the past—not to mention the bedpost!

SACHI MIZUNO
SHINJUKU NIGHTS
$6.50/493-3
A tour through the lives and libidos of the seductive East. No one is better than Sachi Mizuno at weaving an intricate web of sensual desire, wherein many characters are ensnared and enraptured by the demands of their carnal natures.
PASSION IN TOKYO
$6.50/454-2
Tokyo—one of Asia's most historic and seductive cities. Come behind the closed doors of its citizens, and witness the many pleasures that await. Lusty men and women from every stratum of Japanese society free themselves of all inhibitions....

MARTINE GLOWINSKI
POINT OF VIEW
$6.50/433-X
The story of one woman's extraordinary erotic awakening. With the assistance of her new, unexpectedly kinky lover, she discovers and explores her exhibitionist tendencies—until there is virtually nothing she won't do before the horny audiences her man arranges! Unabashed acting out for the sophisticated voyeur.

RICHARD McGOWAN
A HARLOT OF VENUS
$6.50/425-9
A highly fanciful, epic tale of lust on Mars! Cavortia—the most famous and sought-after courtesan in the cosmopolitan city of Venus—finds love and much more during her adventures with some of the most remarkable characters in recent erotic fiction.

M. ORLANDO
THE ARCHITECTURE OF DESIRE
Introduction by Richard Manton.
$6.50/490-9
Two novels in one special volume! In *The Hotel Justine*, an elite clientele is afforded the opportunity to have any and all desires satisfied. *The Villa Sin* is inherited by a beautiful woman who soon realizes that the legacy of the ancestral estate includes bizarre erotic ceremonies. Two pieces of prime real estate.

CHET ROTHWELL
KISS ME, KATHERINE
$5.95/410-0
Beautiful Katherine can hardly believe her luck. Not only is she married to the charming and oh-so-agreeable Nelson, she's free to live out all her erotic fantasies with other men. Katherine's desires are more than any one man can handle—luckily there are always plenty of men on hand, reading and willing to please her!

MARCO VASSI
THE STONED APOCALYPSE
$5.95/401-1/mass market
"Marco Vassi is our champion sexual energist." —*VLS*

During his lifetime, Marco Vassi was praised by writers as diverse as Gore Vidal and Norman Mailer, and his reputation was worldwide. *The Stoned Apocalypse* is Vassi's autobiography; chronicling a cross-country trip on America's erotic byways, it offers a rare glimpse of a generation's sexual imagination.

MASQUERADE BOOKS

ROBIN WILDE
TABITHA'S TICKLE
$6.50/468-2

Tabitha's back! The story of this vicious vixen didn't end with *Tabitha's Tease*. Once again, men fall under the spell of scrumptious co-eds and find themselves enslaved to demands and desires they never dreamed existed. Think it's a man's world? Guess again. With Tabitha around, no man gets what he wants until she's completely satisfied....

ERICA BRONTE
PIRATE'S SLAVE
$5.95/376-7

Lovely young Erica is stranded in a country where lust knows no bounds. Desperate to escape, she finds herself trading her firm, luscious body to any and all men willing and able to help her. Her adventure has its ups and downs, ins and outs—all to the pleasure of lusty Erica!

CHARLES G. WOOD
HELLFIRE
$5.95/358-9

A vicious murderer is running amok in New York's sexual underground—and Nick O'Shay, a virile detective with the NYPD, plunges deep into the case. He soon becomes embroiled in an elusive world of fleshly extremes, hunting a madman seeking to purge America with fire and blood sacrifices. Set in New York's infamous sexual underground.

CLAIRE BAEDER, EDITOR
LA DOMME: A Dominatrix Anthology
$5.95/366-X

A steamy smorgasbord of female domination! Erotic literature has long been filled with heart-stopping portraits of domineering women, and now the most memorable have been brought together in one beautifully brutal volume.

CHARISSE VAN DER LYN
SEX ON THE NET
$5.95/399-6

Electrifying erotica from one of the Internet's hottest and most widely read authors. Encounters of all kinds—straight, lesbian, dominant/submissive and all sorts of extreme passions—are explored in thrilling detail.

STANLEY CARTEN
NAUGHTY MESSAGE
$5.95/333-3

Wesley Arthur discovers a lascivious message on his answering machine. Aroused beyond his wildest dreams by the acts described, Wesley becomes obsessed with tracking down the woman behind the seductive voice. His search takes him through strip clubs, sex parlors and no-tell motels—and finally to his randy reward....

AKBAR DEL PIOMBO
DUKE COSIMO
$4.95/3052-0

A kinky romp played out against the boudoirs, bathrooms and ballrooms of the European nobility, who seem to do nothing all day except each other. The lifestyles of the rich and licentious are revealed in all their glory.
A CRUMBLING FAÇADE
$4.95/3043-1

The return of that incorrigible rogue, Henry Pike, who continues his pursuit of sex, fair or otherwise, in the most elegant homes of the most debauched aristocrats.

CAROLE REMY
FANTASY IMPROMPTU
$6.50/513-1

Kidnapped and held in a remote island retreat, Chantal—a renowned erotic writer—finds herself catering to every sexual whim of the mysterious and arousing Bran. Bran is determined to bring Chantal to a full embracing of her sensual nature, even while revealing himself to be something far more than human....
BEAUTY OF THE BEAST
$5.95/332-5

A shocking tell-all, written from the point-of-view of a prize-winning reporter. And what reporting she does! All the secrets of an uninhibited life are revealed, and each lusty tableau is painted in glowing colors.

DAVID AARON CLARK
THE MARQUIS DE SADE'S JULIETTE
$4.95/240-X

The Marquis de Sade's infamous Juliette returns—and emerges as the most perverse and destructive nightstalker modern New York will ever know. One by one, the innocent are drawn in by Juliette's empty promise of immortality, only to fall prey to her deadly lusts.

ANONYMOUS
LOVE'S ILLUSION
$6.95/549-2

Elizabeth Renard yearned for the body of rich and successful Dan Harrington. Then she discovered Harrington's secret weakness: a need to be humiliated and punished. She makes him her slave, and together they commence a journey into depravity that leaves nothing to the imagination—nothing!
NADIA
$5.95/267-1

Follow the delicious but neglected Nadia as she works to wring every drop of pleasure out of life—despite an unhappy marriage. A classic title providing a peek into the secret sexual lives of another time and place.

MASQUERADE BOOKS

NIGEL McPARR
THE TRANSFORMATION OF EMILY
$6.50/519-0
The shocking story of Emily Johnson, live-in domestic. Without warning, Emily finds herself dismissed by her mistress, and sent to serve at Lilac Row—the home of Charles and Harriet Godwin. In no time, Harriet has Emily doing things she'd never dreamed would be required of her—all involving shocking erotic discipline.

TITIAN BERESFORD
CINDERELLA
$6.50/500-X
Beresford triumphs again with this intoxicating tale, filled with castle dungeons and tightly corseted ladies-in-waiting, naughty viscounts and impossibly cruel masturbatrixes—nearly every conceivable method of erotic torture is explored and described in lush, vivid detail.

JUDITH BOSTON
$6.50/525-5
Edward would have been lucky to get the stodgy companion he thought his parents had hired for him. But an exquisite woman arrives at his door, and Edward finds his lewd behavior never goes unpunished by the unflinchingly severe Judith Boston

NINA FOXTON
$5.95/443-7
An aristocrat finds herself bored by run-of-the-mill amusements for "ladies of good breeding." Instead of taking tea with proper gentlemen, naughty Nina "milks" them of their most private essences. No man ever says "No" to Nina!

P. N. DEDEAUX
THE NOTHING THINGS
$5.95/404-6
Beta Beta Rho has taken on a new group of pledges. The five women will be put through the most grueling of ordeals, and punished severely for any shortcomings. Before long, all Beta pledges come to crave their punishments—and eagerly await next year's crop!

LYN DAVENPORT
THE GUARDIAN II
$6.50/505-0
The tale of submissive Felicia Brookes continues in this volume of sensual surprises. No sooner has Felicia come to love Rodney than she discovers that she must now accustom herself to the guardianship of the debauched Duke of Smithton. Surely Rodney will rescue her from the domination of this stranger. Won't he?

DOVER ISLAND
$5.95/384-8
Dr. David Kelly has planted the seeds of his dream—a Corporal Punishment Resort. Soon, many people from varied walks of life descend upon this isolated retreat, intent on fulfilling their every desire. Including Marcy Harris, the perfect partner for the lustful Doctor....

LIZBETH DUSSEAU
THE APPLICANT
$6.50/501-8
"Adventuresome young women who enjoys being submissive sought by married couple in early forties. Expect no limits." Hilary answers an ad, hoping to find someone who can meet her special needs. The beautiful Liza turns out to be a flawless mistress, and together with her husband, Oliver, she trains Hilary to be the perfect servant—much to Hilary's delight and arousal!

ANTHONY BOBARZYNSKI
STASI SLUT
$4.95/3050-4
Adina lives in East Germany, where she can only dream about the freedoms of the West. But then she meets a group of ruthless and corrupt STASI agents. They use her body for their own perverse gratification, while she opts to use her talents in a final bid for total freedom!

JOCELYN JOYCE
PRIVATE LIVES
$4.95/309-0
The lecherous habits of the illustrious make for a sizzling tale of French erotic life. A widow has a craving for a young busboy; he's sleeping with a rich businessman's wife; her husband is minding his sex business elsewhere! Sexual entanglements run through this tale of upper crust lust!

SARAH JACKSON
SANCTUARY
$5.95/318-X
Sanctuary explores both the unspeakable debauchery of court life and the unimaginable privations of monastic solitude, leading the voracious and the virtuous on a collision course that brings history to throbbing life.

THE WILD HEART
$4.95/3007-5
A luxury hotel is the setting for this artful web of sex, desire, and love. A newlywed sees sex as a duty, while her hungry husband tries to awaken her to its tender joys. A Parisian entertains wealthy guests for the love of money. Each episode provides a new variation in this lusty Grand Hotel!

MASQUERADE BOOKS

MASQUERADE BOOKS

THE BEST OF PAUL LITTLE
$6.50/469-0

Known throughout the world for his fantastic portrayals of punishment and pleasure, Little never fails to push readers over the edge of sensual excitement.

ALL THE WAY
$6.95/509-3

Two excruciating novels from Paul Little in one hot volume! *Going All the Way* features an unhappy man who tries to purge himself of the memory of his lover with a series of quirky and uninhibited lovers. *Pushover* tells the story of a serial spanker and his celebrated exploits.

THE DISCIPLINE OF ODETTE
$5.95/334-1

Odette was sure marriage would rescue her from her family's "corrections." To her horror, she discovers that her beloved has also been raised on discipline. A shocking erotic coupling!

THE PRISONER
$5.95/330-9

Judge Black has built a secret room below a penitentiary, where he sentences the prisoners to hours of exhibition and torment while his friends watch. Judge Black's brand of rough justice keeps his lovely young captives on the brink of utter pleasure!

TEARS OF THE INQUISITION
$4.95/146-2

A staggering account of pleasure and punishment. "There was a tickling inside her as her nervous system reminded her she was ready for sex. But before her was...the Inquisitor!"

DOUBLE NOVEL
$4.95/86-6

The Metamorphosis of Lisette Joyaux tells the story of a young woman initiated into an incredible world world of lesbian lusts. *The Story of Monique* reveals the twisted sexual rituals that beckon the ripe and willing Monique.

CAPTIVE MAIDENS
$5.95/440-2

Three beautiful/young women find themselves powerless against the debauched landowners of 1824 England. They are banished to a sexual slave colony, and corrupted by every imaginable perversion.

SLAVE ISLAND
$5.95/441-0

A leisure cruise is waylaid by Lord Henry Philbrock, a sadistic genius. The ship's passengers are kidnapped and spirited to his island prison, where the women are trained to accommodate the most bizarre sexual cravings of the rich, the famous, the pampered and the perverted.

ALIZARIN LAKE

CLARA
$6.95/548-4

The mysterious death of a beautiful, aristocratic woman leads her old boyfriend on a harrowing journey of discovery. His search uncovers a woman on a quest for deeper and more unusual sensations, each more shocking than the one before!

SEX ON DOCTOR'S ORDERS
$5.95/402-X

Beth, a nubile young nurse, uses her considerable skills to further medical science by offering incomparable and insatiable assistance in the gathering of important specimens. Soon, an assortment of randy characters is lending a hand—and more!

THE EROTIC ADVENTURES OF HARRY TEMPLE
$4.95/127-6

Harry Temple's memoirs chronicle his amorous adventures from his initiation at the hands of insatiable sirens, through his stay at a house of hot repute, to his encounters with a chastity-belted nympho!

JOHN NORMAN

TARNSMAN OF GOR
$6.95/486-0

This controversial series returns! Tarl Cabot is transported to Gor. He must quickly accustom himself to the ways of this world, including the caste system which exalts some as Priest-Kings or Warriors, and debases others as slaves. A spectacular world unfolds in this first volume of John Norman's Gorean series.

OUTLAW OF GOR
$6.95/487-9

In this second volume, Tarl Cabot returns to Gor, where he might reclaim both his woman and his role of Warrior. But upon arriving, he discovers that his name, his city and the names of those he loves have become unspeakable. Cabot has become an outlaw, and must discover his new purpose on this strange planet, where danger stalks the outcast, and even simple answers have their price....

PRIEST-KINGS OF GOR
$6.95/488-7

Tarl Cabot searches for the truth about his lovely wife Talena. Does she live, or was she destroyed by the mysterious, all-powerful Priest-Kings? Cabot is determined to find out—even while knowing that no one who has approached the mountain stronghold of the Priest-Kings has ever returned alive....

BUY ANY 4 BOOKS & CHOOSE 1 ADDITIONAL BOOK, OF EQUAL OR LESSER VALUE, AS YOUR FREE GIFT

MASQUERADE BOOKS

NOMADS OF GOR
$6.95/527-1

Another provocative trip to the barbaric and mysterious world of Gor. Norman's heroic Tarnsman finds his way across this Counter-Earth, pledged to serve the Priest-Kings in their quest for survival. Unfortunately for Cabot, his mission leads him to the savage Wagon People—nomads who may very well kill before surrendering any secrets....

SYDNEY ST. JAMES
RIVE GAUCHE
$5.95/317-1

The Latin Quarter, Paris, circa 1920. Expatriate bohemians couple with abandon—before eventually abandoning their ambitions amidst the intoxicating temptations waiting to be indulged in every bedroom.

GARDEN OF DELIGHT
$4.95/3058-X

A vivid account of sexual awakening that follows an innocent but insatiably curious young woman's journey from the furtive, forbidden joys of dormitory life to the unabashed carnality of the wild world.

DON WINSLOW
THE FALL OF THE ICE QUEEN
$6.50/520-4

She was the most exquisite of his courtiers: the beautiful, aloof woman who Rahn the Conqueror chose as his Consort. But the regal disregard with which she treated Rahn was not to be endured. It was decided that she would submit to his will, and learn to serve her lord in the fashion he had come to expect. And as so many had learned, Rahn's depraved expectations have made his court infamous....

PRIVATE PLEASURES
$6.50/504-2

An assortment of sensual encounters designed to appeal to the most discerning reader. Frantic voyeurs, licentious exhibitionists, and everyday lovers are here displayed in all their wanton glory—proving again that fleshly pleasures have no more apt chronicler than Don Winslow.

THE INSATIABLE MISTRESS OF ROSEDALE
$6.50/494-1

The story of the perfect couple: Edward and Lady Penelope, who reside in beautiful and mysterious Rosedale manor. While Edward is a true connoisseur of sexual perversion, it is Lady Penelope whose mastery of complete sensual pleasure makes their home infamous. Indulging one another's bizarre whims is a way of life for this wicked couple, and none who encounter the extravagances of Rosedale will forget what they've learned....

SECRETS OF CHEATEM MANOR
$6.50/434-8

Edward returns to his late father's estate, to find it being run by the majestic Lady Amanda. Edward can hardly believe his luck—Lady Amanda is assisted by her two beautiful, lonely daughters, Catherine and Prudence. What the randy young man soon comes to realize is the love of discipline that all three beauties share.

KATERINA IN CHARGE
$5.95/409-7

When invited to a country retreat by a mysterious couple, two randy young ladies can hardly resist! But do they have any idea what they're in for? Whatever the case, the imperious Katerina will make her desires known very soon— and demand that they be fulfilled... A thoroughly perverse tale of ultimate sensual innocence subjugated and defiled by one powerful woman.

THE MANY PLEASURES OF IRONWOOD
$5.95/310-4

Seven lovely young women are employed by The Ironwood Sportsmen's Club, where their natural talents in the sensual arts are put to creative use. A small and exclusive club with seven carefully selected sexual connoisseurs, Ironwood is dedicated to the relentless pursuit of forbidden pleasures.

CLAIRE'S GIRLS
$5.95/442-9

You knew when she walked by that she was something special. She was one of Claire's girls, a woman carefully dressed and groomed to fill a role, to capture a look, to fit an image crafted by the sophisticated proprietress of an exclusive escort agency. High-class whores blow the roof off in this blow-by-blow account of life behind the closed doors of a sophisticated brothel.

N. WHALLEN
TAU'TEVU
$6.50/426-7

In a mysterious and exotic land, the statuesque and beautiful Vivian learns to subject herself to the hand of a strange and domineering man. He systematically helps her prove her own strength, and brings to life in her an unimagined sensual fire.

THE CLASSIC COLLECTION
PROTESTS, PLEASURES, RAPTURES
$5.95/400-3

Invited for an allegedly quiet weekend at a country vicarage, a young woman is stunned to find herself surrounded by shocking acts of sexual sadism. Soon her curiosity is piqued, and she begins to explore her own capacities for delicious sexual cruelty.

MASQUERADE BOOKS

THE YELLOW ROOM
$5.95/378-3
The "yellow room" holds the secrets of lust, lechery, and the lash. There, bare-bottomed, spread-eagled, and open to the world, demure Alice Darvell soon learns to love her lickings.

SCHOOL DAYS IN PARIS
$5.95/325-2
The rapturous chronicles of a well-spent youth! Few Universities provide the profound and pleasurable lessons one learns in after-hours study—particularly if one is young and available, and lucky enough to have Paris as a playground.

MAN WITH A MAID
$4.95/307-4
The adventures of Jack and Alice have delighted readers for eight decades! A classic of its genre, *Man with a Maid* tells an outrageous tale of desire, revenge, and submission. Over 200,000 copies in print!

CLASSIC EROTIC BIOGRAPHIES
JENNIFER III
$5.95/292-2
The adventures of erotica's most daring heroine. Jennifer has a photographer's eye for details—particularly of the male variety! One by one, her subjects submit to her demands for pleasure.

RHINOCEROS

KATHLEEN K.
SWEET TALKERS
$6.95/516-6
"If you enjoy eavesdropping on explicit conversations about sex... this book is for you."   —*Spectator*

Kathleen K. ran a phone-sex company in the late 80s, and she opens up her diary for a very thought provoking peek at the life of a phone-sex operator. Transcripts of actual conversations are included.
Trade /$12.95/192-6

THOMAS S. ROCHE
DARK MATTER
$6.95/484-4
"*Dark Matter* is sure to please gender outlaws, bodymod junkies, goth vampires, boys who wish they were dykes, and anybody who's not to sure where the fine line should be drawn between pleasure and pain. It's a handful."—Pat Califia

"Here is the erotica of the cumming millennium.... You will be deliciously disturbed, but never disappointed."
—Poppy Z. Brite

NOIROTICA: An Anthology of Erotic Crime Stories (Ed.)
$6.95/390-2
A collection of darkly sexy tales, taking place at the crossroads of the crime and erotic genres. Thomas S. Roche has gathered together some of today's finest writers of sexual fiction, all of whom explore the murky terrain where desire runs irrevocably afoul of the law.

ROMY ROSEN
SPUNK
$6.95/492-5
Casey, a lovely model poised upon the verge of super-celebrity, falls for an insatiable young rock singer—not suspecting that his sexual appetite has led him to experiment with a dangerous new aphrodisiac. Soon, Casey becomes addicted to the drug, and her craving plunges her into a strange underworld, where the only chance for redemption lies with a shadowy young man with a secret of his own.

MOLLY WEATHERFIELD
CARRIE'S STORY
$6.95/485-2
"I was stunned by how well it was written and how intensely foreign I found its sexual world.... And, since this is a world I don't frequent... I thoroughly enjoyed the National Geo tour."
—*bOING bOING*

"Hilarious and harrowing... just when you think things can't get any wilder, they do."   —*Black Sheets*

"I had been Jonathan's slave for about a year when he told me he wanted to sell me at an auction. I wasn't in any condition to respond when he told me this…" Desire and depravity run rampant in this story of uncompromising mastery and irrevocable submission. A unique piece of erotica that is both thoughtful and hot!

CYBERSEX CONSORTIUM
CYBERSEX: The Perv's Guide to Finding Sex on the Internet
$6.95/471-2
You've heard the objections: cyberspace is soaked with sex, mired in immorality. Okay—so where is it!? Tracking down the good stuff—the real good stuff—can waste an awful lot of expensive time, and frequently leave you high and dry. The Cybersex Consortium presents an easy-to-use guide for those intrepid adults who know what they want. No horny hacker can afford to pass up this map to the kinkiest rest stops on the Info Superhighway.

BUY ANY 4 BOOKS & CHOOSE 1 ADDITIONAL BOOK, OF EQUAL OR LESSER VALUE, AS YOUR FREE GIFT

MASQUERADE BOOKS

AMELIA G, EDITOR
BACKSTAGE PASSES
$6.95/438-0

Amelia G, editor of the goth-sex journal *Blue Blood*, has brought together some of today's most irreverent writers, each of whom has outdone themselves with an edgy, antic tale of modern lust. Punks, metalheads, and grunge-trash roam the pages of *Backstage Passes*, and no one knows their ways better...

GERI NETTICK
WITH BETH ELLIOT
MIRRORS: PORTRAIT OF A LESBIAN TRANSSEXUAL
$6.95/435-6

The alternately heartbreaking and empowering story of one woman's long road to full selfhood. Born a male, Geri Nettick knew something just didn't fit. And even after coming to terms with her own gender dysphoria—and taking steps to correct it—she still fought to be accepted by the lesbian feminist community to which she felt she belonged. A true tale of struggle and discovery.

DAVID MELTZER
UNDER
$6.95/290-6

The story of a 21st century sex professional living at the bottom of the social heap. After surgeries designed to increase his physical allure, corrupt government forces drive the cyber-gigolo underground—where even more bizarre cultures await him.

ORF
$6.95/110-1

He is the ultimate musician-hero—the idol of thousands, the fevered dream of many more. And like many musicians before him, he is misunderstood, misused—and totally out of control. Every last drop of feeling is squeezed from a modern-day troubadour and his lady love.

LAURA ANTONIOU, EDITOR
NO OTHER TRIBUTE
$6.95/294-9

A collection sure to challenge Political Correctness in a way few have before, with tales of women kept in bondage to their lovers by their deepest passions. Love pushes these women beyond acceptable limits, rendering them helpless to deny anything to the men and women they adore.

SOME WOMEN
$6.95/300-7

Over forty essays written by women actively involved in consensual dominance and submission. Pro doms, lifestyle leatherdykes, titleholders—women from every walk of life lay bare their true feelings about explosive issues.

BY HER SUBDUED
$6.95/281-7

These tales all involve women in control—of their lives, their loves, their men. So much in control that they can remorselessly break rules to become powerful goddesses of the men who sacrifice all to worship at their feet.

TRISTAN TAORMINO &
DAVID AARON CLARK, EDS.
RITUAL SEX
$6.95/391-0

The many contributors to *Ritual Sex* know—and demonstrate—that body and soul share more common ground than society feels comfortable acknowledging. From personal memoirs of ecstatic revelation, to fictional quests to reconcile sex and spirit, *Ritual Sex* provides an unprecedented look at private life. One of today's most challenging anthologies.

TAMMY JO ECKHART
PUNISHMENT FOR THE CRIME
$6.95/427-5

The first collection from this emerging talent. Peopled by characters of rare depth, these stories explore the true meaning of dominance and submission. From an encounter between two of society's most despised individuals, to the explorations of longtime friends, these tales take you where few others have ever dared....

AMARANTHA KNIGHT, ED.
SEDUCTIVE SPECTRES
$6.95/464-X

Breathtaking tours through the erotic supernatural via the macabre imaginations of today's best writers. Never before have ghostly encounters been so alluring, thanks to a cast of otherworldly characters well-acquainted with the pleasures of the flesh.

SEX MACABRE
$6.95/392-9

Horror tales designed for dark and sexy nights. Amarantha Knight—the woman behind the Darker Passions series—has gathered together erotic stories sure to make your skin crawl, and heart beat faster. A thrilling collection, and an important volume in the growing field of erotic horror.

FLESH FANTASTIC
$6.95/352-X

Humans have long toyed with the idea of "playing God": creating life from nothingness, bringing life to the inanimate. Now Amarantha Knight collects stories exploring not only the act of Creation, but the lust that follows. Includes work by some of today's edgiest writers.

MASQUERADE BOOKS

GARY BOWEN
DIARY OF A VAMPIRE
$6.95/331-7

"Gifted with a darkly sensual vision and a fresh voice, [Bowen] is a writer to watch out for."
—Cecilia Tan

Rafael, a red-blooded male with an insatiable hunger for the same, is the perfect antidote to the effete malcontents haunting bookstores today. The emergence of a bold and brilliant vision, rooted in past and present.

RENÉ MAIZEROY
FLESHLY ATTRACTIONS
$6.95/299-X

Lucien was the son of the wantonly beautiful actress, Marie-Rose Hardanges. When she decides to let a "friend" introduce her son to the pleasures of love, Marie-Rose could not have foretold the excesses that would lead to her own ruin and that of her cherished son.

JEAN STINE
THRILL CITY
$6.95/411-9

Thrill City is the seat of the world's increasing depravity, and this classic novel transports you there with a vivid style you'd be hard pressed to ignore. No writer is better suited to describe the extremes of this modern Babylon.

SEASON OF THE WITCH
$6.95/268-X

"A future in which it is technically possible to transfer the total mind...of a rapist killer into the brain dead but physically living body of his female victim. Remarkable for intense psychological technique. There is eroticism but it is necessary to mark the differences between the sexes and the subtle altering of a man into a woman."
—The Science Fiction Critic

GRANT ANTREWS
ROGUE'S GALLERY
$6.95/522-0

A stirring evocation of dominant/submissive love. Two doctors meet and slowly fall in love. Once Beth reveals her hidden desires to Jim, the two explore the forbidden acts that will come to define their distinctly exotic affair.

JOHN WARREN
THE TORQUEMADA KILLER
$6.95/367-8

Detective Eva Hernandez gets her first "big case": a string of vicious murders taking place within New York's SM community. Eva assembles the evidence, revealing a picture of a world misunderstood and under attack—and gradually comes to understand her own place within it.

THE LOVING DOMINANT
$6.95/218-3

Everything you need to know about an infamous sexual variation—and an unspoken type of love. Warren guides readers through this world and reveals the too-often hidden basis of the D/S relationship: care, trust and love.

LAURA ANTONIOU
writing as "Sara Adamson"
THE TRAINER
$6.95/249-3

The Marketplace includes not only willing slaves, but the exquisite trainers who take submissives firmly in hand. And now these mentors divulge the desires that led them to become the ultimate figures of authority.

THE SLAVE
$6.95/173-X

One talented submissive longs to join the ranks of those who have proven themselves worthy of entry into the Marketplace. But the delicious price is high....

THE MARKETPLACE
$6.95/3096-2

The volume that introduced the Marketplace to the world—and established it as one of the most popular realms in contemporary SM fiction.

DAVID AARON CLARK
SISTER RADIANCE
$6.95/215-9

A meditation on love, sex, and death, rife with Clark's trademark vivisections of contemporary desires, sacred and profane. The vicissitudes of lust and romance are examined against a backdrop of urban decay in this testament to the allure—and inevitability—of the forbidden.

THE WET FOREVER
$6.95/117-9

The story of Janus and Madchen—a small-time hood and a beautiful sex worker on the run from one of the most dangerous men they have ever known—examines themes of loyalty, sacrifice, redemption and obsession amidst Manhattan's sex parlors and underground S/M clubs. A thrillingly contemporary love story.

MICHAEL PERKINS
EVIL COMPANIONS
$6.95/3067-9

Set in New York City during the tumultuous waning years of the Sixties, Evil Companions has been hailed as "a frightening classic." A young couple explores the nether reaches of the erotic unconscious in a shocking confrontation with the extremes of passion.

BUY ANY 4 BOOKS & CHOOSE 1 ADDITIONAL BOOK, OF EQUAL OR LESSER VALUE, AS YOUR FREE GIFT

MASQUERADE BOOKS

THE SECRET RECORD:
Modern Erotic Literature
$6.95/3039-3

Michael Perkins surveys the field with authority and unique insight. Updated and revised to include the latest trends, tastes, and developments in this misunderstood and maligned genre.

AN ANTHOLOGY OF CLASSIC ANONYMOUS EROTIC WRITING
$6.95/140-3

Michael Perkins has collected the very best passages from the world's erotic writing. "Anonymous" is one of the most infamous bylines in publishing history—and these steamy excerpts show why!

LIESEL KULIG
LOVE IN WARTIME
$6.95/3044-X

Madeleine knew that the handsome SS officer was a dangerous man, but she was just a cabaret singer in Nazi-occupied Paris, trying to survive in a perilous time. When Josef fell in love with her, he discovered that a beautiful woman can sometimes be as dangerous as any warrior.

HELEN HENLEY
ENTER WITH TRUMPETS
$6.95/197-7

Helen Henley was told that women just don't write about sex—much less the taboos she was so interested in exploring. So Henley did it alone, flying in the face of "tradition" by writing this touching tale of arousal and devotion in one couple's kinky relationship.

ALICE JOANOU
BLACK TONGUE
$6.95/258-2

"Joanou has created a series of sumptuous, brooding, dark visions of sexual obsession, and is undoubtedly a name to look out for in the future." —*Redeemer*

Exploring lust at its most florid and unsparing, *Black Tongue* is a trove of baroque fantasies—each redolent of forbidden passions. Joanou creates some of erotica's most mesmerizing and unforgettable characters.

TOURNIQUET
$6.95/3060-1

A heady collection of stories and effusions from the pen of one our most dazzling young writers. Strange tales abound in this complex and riveting series of meditations on desire.

CANNIBAL FLOWER
$4.95/72-6

"She is waiting in her darkened bedroom, as she has waited throughout history, to seduce the men who are foolish enough to be blinded by her irresistible charms.... She is the goddess of sexuality, and *Cannibal Flower* is her haunting siren song." —Michael Perkins

PHILIP JOSÉ FARMER
A FEAST UNKNOWN
$6.95/276-0

"Sprawling, brawling, shocking, suspenseful, hilarious..." —Theodore Sturgeon

Farmer's supreme anti-hero returns. "I was conceived and born in 1888." Slowly, Lord Grandrith—armed with the belief that he is the son of Jack the Ripper—tells the story of his remarkable and unbridled life. His story begins with his discovery of the secret of immortality—and progresses to encompass the furthest extremes of human behavior.

DANIEL VIAN
ILLUSIONS
$6.95/3074-1

International lust. Two tales of danger and desire in Berlin on the eve of WWII. From private homes to lurid cafés, passion is exposed in stark contrast to the brutal violence of the time, as desperate people explore their darkest sexual desires.

SAMUEL R. DELANY
THE MAD MAN
$8.99/408-9

"Reads like a pornographic reflection of Peter Ackroyd's *Chatterton* or A. S. Byatt's *Possession*.... Delany develops an insightful dichotomy between [his protagonist]'s two worlds: the one of cerebral philosophy and dry academia, the other of heedless, 'impersonal' obsessive sexual extremism. When these worlds finally collide...the novel achieves a surprisingly satisfying resolution...." —*Publishers Weekly*

Graduate student John Marr researches the life of Timothy Hasler: a philosopher whose career was cut tragically short over a decade earlier. On another front, Marr finds himself increasingly drawn toward shocking, depraved sexual entanglements with the homeless men of his neighborhood, until it begins to seem that Hasler's death might hold some key to his own life as a gay man in the age of AIDS.

ANDREI CODRESCU
THE REPENTANCE OF LORRAINE
$6.95/329-5

"One of our most prodigiously talented and magical writers." —*NYT Book Review*

By the acclaimed author of *The Hole in the Flag* and *The Blood Countess*. An aspiring writer, a professor's wife, a secretary, gold anklets, Maoists, Roman harlots—and more—swirl through this spicy tale of a harried quest for a mythic artifact. Written when the author was a young man, this lusty yarn was inspired by the heady days of the Sixties. Includes a new introduction by the author, detailing the events that inspired *Lorraine*'s creation. A touching, arousing product from a more innocent time.

MASQUERADE BOOKS

TUPPY OWENS
SENSATIONS
$6.95/3081-4

Tuppy Owens tells the unexpurgated story of the making of *Sensations*—the first big-budget sex flick. Originally commissioned to appear in book form after the release of the film in 1975, *Sensations* is finally released under Masquerade's stylish *Rhinoceros* imprint.

SOPHIE GALLEYMORE BIRD
MANEATER
$6.95/103-9

Through a bizarre act of creation, a man attains the "perfect" lover—by all appearances a beautiful, sensuous woman, but in reality something far darker. Once brought to life she will accept no mate, seeking instead the prey that will sate her hunger for vengeance.

LEOPOLD VON SACHER-MASOCH
VENUS IN FURS
$6.95/3089-X

The first uncompromising exploration of the dominant/submissive relationship in literature. The alliance of Severin and Wanda epitomizes Sacher-Masoch's dark obsession with a cruel, controlling goddess and the urges that drive the man held in her thrall.

BADBOY

KITTY TSUI WRITING AS ERIC NORTON
SPARKS FLY
$6.95/551-4

The acclaimed author of *Breathless* explores the highest highs—and most wretched lows—of life as Eric Norton, a beautiful wanton living San Francisco's high life. *Sparks Fly* traces Norton's rise, fall, and resurrection, vividly marking the way with the personal affairs that give life meaning. Scaldingly hot and totally revealing.

MICHAEL FORD, EDITOR
BUTCH BOYS:
Stories For Men Who Need It Bad
$6.50/523-9

A big volume of tales dedicated to the rough-and-tumble type who can make a man weak at the knees. Some of today's best erotic writers explore the many possible variations on the age-old fantasy of the dominant man.

WILLIAM J. MANN, EDITOR
GRAVE PASSIONS:
Gay Tales of the Supernatural
$6.50/405-4

A collection of the most chilling tales of passion currently being penned by today's most provocative gay writers. Unnatural transformations, otherworldly encounters, and deathless desires make for a collection sure to keep readers up late at night—for a variety of reasons!

J. A. GUERRA, EDITOR
COME QUICKLY:
For Boys on the Go
$6.50/413-5

Here are over sixty of the hottest fantasies around—all designed to get you going in less time than it takes to dial 976. Julian Anthony Guerra, the editor behind the popular *Men at Work* and *Badboy Fantasies*, has put together this volume especially for you—a busy man on a modern schedule, who still appreciates a little old-fashioned action. Hassle- free quickies.

JOHN PRESTON
HUSTLING: A Gentleman's Guide to the Fine Art of Homosexual Prostitution
$6.50/517-4

"...Unrivaled. For any man even vaguely contemplating going into business this tome has got to be the first port of call."
—*Divinity*

"Fun and highly literary. What more could you expect form such an accomplished activist, author and editor?" —*Drummer*

The very first guide to the gay world's most infamous profession. John Preston solicited the advice and opinions of "working boys" from across the country in his effort to produce the ultimate guide to the hustler's world. *Hustling* covers every practical aspect of the business, from clientele and payment options to "specialties," sidelines and drawbacks. No stone is left unturned in this guidebook to the ins and outs of this much-mythologized—and largely misunderstood—trade.
Trade $12.95/137-3

MR. BENSON
$4.95/3041-5

Jamie is an aimless young man lucky enough to encounter Mr. Benson. He is soon led down the path of erotic enlightenment, learning to accept this man as his master. Jamie's incredible adventures never fail to excite—especially when the going gets rough!

MASQUERADE BOOKS

TALES FROM THE DARK LORD
$5.95/323-6
A new collection of twelve stunning works from the man *Lambda Book Report* called "the Dark Lord of gay erotica." The relentless ritual of lust and surrender is explored in all its manifestations in this heart-stopping triumph of authority and vision from the Dark Lord!

TALES FROM THE DARK LORD II
$4.95/176-4
The second volume of John Preston's masterful short stories.

THE ARENA
$4.95/3083-0
There is a place on the edge of fantasy where every desire is indulged with abandon. Men go there to unleash beasts, to let demons roam free, to abolish all limits. At the center of each tale are the men who serve there, who offer themselves for the consummation of any passion, whose own urges compel their endless sub-servience.

THE HEIR·THE KING
$4.95/3048-5
The ground-breaking novel *The Heir*, written in the lyric voice of the ancient myths, tells the story of a world where slaves and masters create a new sexual society. *The King* tells the story of a soldier who discovers his monarch's most secret desires. A special double volume.

THE MISSION OF ALEX KANE
SWEET DREAMS
$4.95/3062-8
It's the triumphant return of gay action hero Alex Kane! In *Sweet Dreams*, Alex travels to Boston where he takes on a street gang that stalks gay teenagers. Mighty Alex Kane wreaks a fierce and terrible vengeance on those who prey on gay people everywhere!

GOLDEN YEARS
$4.95/3069-5
When evil threatens the plans of a group of older gay men, Kane's got the muscle to take it head on. Along the way, he wins the support—and very specialized attentions—of a cowboy plucked right out of the Old West.

DEADLY LIES
$4.95/3076-8
Politics is a dirty business and the dirt becomes deadly when a political smear campaign targets gay men. Who better to clean things up than Alex Kane! Alex comes to protect the lives of gay men imperiled by lies and deceit.

STOLEN MOMENTS
$4.95/3098-9
Houston's evolving gay community is victimized by a malicious newspaper editor who is more than willing to sacrifice gays on the altar of circulation. He never counted on Alex Kane, fearless defender of gay dreams and desires.

SECRET DANGER
$4.95/111-X
Homophobia: a pernicious social ill not confined by America's borders. Alex Kane and the faithful Danny are called to a small European country, where a group of gay tourists is being held hostage by ruthless terrorists. Luckily, the Mission of Alex Kane stands as firm foreign policy.

LETHAL SILENCE
$4.95/125-0
The Mission of Alex Kane thunders to a conclusion. Chicago becomes the scene of the right-wing's most noxious plan—facilitated by unholy political alliances. Alex and Danny head to the Windy City to take up battle with the mercenaries who would squash gay men underfoot.

•••••••••••••••••••••••••••••••••••

MATT TOWNSEND
SOLIDLY BUILT
$6.50/416-X
The tale of the tumultuous relationship between Jeff, a young photographer, and Mark, the butch electrician hired to wire Jeff's new home. For Jeff, it's love at first sight; Mark, however, has more than a few hang-ups. Soon, both are forced to reevaluate their outlooks, and are assisted by a variety of hot men....

•••••••••••••••••••••••••••••••••••

JAY SHAFFER
SHOOTERS
$5.95/284-1
No mere catalog of random acts, *Shooters* tells the stories of a variety of stunning men and the ways they connect in sexual and non-sexual ways. A virtuoso storyteller, Shaffer always gets his man.

ANIMAL HANDLERS
$4.95/264-7
In Shaffer's world, each and every man finally succumbs to the animal urges deep inside. And if there's any creature that promises a wild time, it's a beast who's been caged for far too long. Shaffer has one of the keenest eyes for the nuances of male passion.

FULL SERVICE
$4.95/150-0
Wild men build up steam until they finally let loose. No-nonsense guys bear down hard on each other as they work their way toward release in this finely detailed assortment of masculine fantasies. One of gay erotica's most insightful chroniclers of male passion.

•••••••••••••••••••••••••••••••••••

D. V. SADERO
IN THE ALLEY
$4.95/144-6
Hardworking men—from cops to carpenters—bring their own special skills and impressive tools to the most satisfying job of all: capturing and breaking the male sexual beast. Hot, incisive and way over the top.

MASQUERADE BOOKS

SCOTT O'HARA

DO-IT-YOURSELF PISTON POLISHING
$6.50/489-5

Longtime sex-pro Scott O'Hara draws upon his acute powers of seduction to lure you into a world of hard, horny men long overdue for a tune-up. Pretty soon, you'll pop your own hood for the servicing you know you need....

SUTTER POWELL

EXECUTIVE PRIVILEGES
$6.50/383-X

No matter how serious or sexy a predicament his characters find themselves in, Powell conveys the sheer exuberance of their encounters with a warm humor rarely seen in contemporary gay erotica.

GARY BOWEN

WESTERN TRAILS
$6.50/477-1

A wild roundup of tales devoted to life on the lone prairie. Gary Bowen—a writer well-versed in the Western genre—has collected the very best contemporary cowboy stories. Some of gay literature's brightest stars tell the sexy truth about the many ways a rugged stud found to satisfy himself—and his buddy—in the Very Wild West.

MAN HUNGRY
$5.95/374-0

By the author of *Diary of a Vampire*. A riveting collection of stories from one of gay erotica's new stars. Dipping into a variety of genres, Bowen crafts tales of lust unlike anything being published today.

KYLE STONE

HOT BAUDS 2
$6.50/479-8

Another collection of cyberfantasies, compiled by the inimitable Kyle Stone. After the success of the original *Hot Bauds*, Stone conducted another heated search through the world's randiest gay bulletin boards, resulting in one of the most scalding follow-ups ever published. Here's all the scandalous stuff you've heard so much about—sexy, shameless, and eminently user-friendly.

FIRE & ICE
$5.95/297-3

A collection of stories from the author of the infamous adventures of PB 500. Randy, powerful, and just plain bad, Stone's characters always promise one thing: enough hot action to burn away your desire for anyone else....

HOT BAUDS
$5.95/285-X

Stone combed cyberspace for the hottest fantasies of the world's horniest hackers. Stone has assembled the first collection of the raunchy erotica so many gay men surf the Net for.

FANTASY BOARD
$4.95/212-4

The author of the scalding sci-fi adventures of PB 500 explores the more foreseeable future—through the intertwined lives (and private parts) of a collection of randy computer hackers. On the Lambda Gate BBS, every hot and horny male is in search of a little virtual satisfaction!

THE CITADEL
$4.95/198-5

The sequel to *The Initiation of PB 500*. Having proven himself worthy of his stunning master, Micah—now known only as '500'—will face new challenges and hardships after his entry into the forbidding Citadel. Only his master knows what awaits—and whether Micah will again distinguish himself as the perfect instrument of pleasure....

THE INITIATION OF PB 500
$4.95/141-1

He is a stranger on their planet, unschooled in their language, and ignorant of their customs. But this man, Micah—now known only by his number—will soon be trained in every detail of erotic service. He must begin proving himself worthy of the master who has chosen him....

RITUALS
$4.95/168-3

Via a computer bulletin board, a young man finds himself drawn into a series of sexual rites that transform him into the willing slave of a mysterious stranger. All vestiges of his former life are thrown off, and he learns to live for his Master's touch....

ROBERT BAHR

SEX SHOW
$4.95/225-6

Luscious dancing boys. Brazen, explicit acts. Take a seat, and get very comfortable, because the curtain's going up on a show no discriminating appetite can afford to miss.

JASON FURY

THE ROPE ABOVE, THE BED BELOW
$4.95/269-8

The irresistible Jason Fury returns—this time, telling the tale of a vicious murderer preying upon New York's go-go boys. In order to solve this mystery and save lives, each studly suspect must lay bare his soul—and more!

BUY ANY 4 BOOKS & CHOOSE 1 ADDITIONAL BOOK, OF EQUAL OR LESSER VALUE, AS YOUR FREE GIFT

MASQUERADE BOOKS

ERIC'S BODY
$4.95/151-9

Fury's sexiest tales are collected in book form for the first time. Follow the irresistible Jason through sexual adventures unlike any you have ever read....

LARS EIGHNER
WHISPERED IN THE DARK
$5.95/286-8

A volume demonstrating Eighner's unique combination of strengths: poetic descriptive power, an unfailing ear for dialogue, and a finely tuned feeling for the nuances of male passion. One of his very best collections.

AMERICAN PRELUDE
$4.95/170-5

Eighner is widely recognized as one of our best, most exciting gay writers. He is also one of gay erotica's true masters—and American Prelude shows why. Wonderfully written, blisteringly hot tales of all-American lust between oversexed studs.

B.M.O.C.
$4.95/3077-6

In a college town known as "the Athens of the Southwest," studs of every stripe are up all night—studying, naturally. Relive university life the way it was supposed to be, with a cast of handsome honor students majoring in Human Homosexuality.

DAVID LAURENTS, EDITOR
SOUTHERN COMFORT
$6.50/466-6

Editor David Laurents now unleashes a collection of tales focusing on the American South—stories reflecting not only Southern literary tradition, but the many sexy contributions the region has made to the iconography of the American Male. Not to be missed.

WANDERLUST: HOMOEROTIC TALES OF TRAVEL
$5.95/395-3

A volume dedicated to the special pleasures of faraway places. Gay men have always had an extraordinary interest in travel—and not only for the scenic vistas. Wanderlust celebrates the freedom of the open road, and the allure of men who stray from the beaten path....

THE BADBOY BOOK OF EROTIC POETRY
$5.95/382-1

Over fifty of today's best poets. Erotic poetry has long been the problem child of the literary world—highly creative and provocative, but somehow too frank to be "literature." The Badboy Book of Erotic Poetry restores eros to its rightful place of honor in contemporary gay writing.

AARON TRAVIS
BIG SHOTS
$5.95/448-8

Two fierce tales in one electrifying volume. In Beirut, Travis tells the story of ultimate military power and erotic subjugation; Kip, Travis' hypersexed and sinister take on film noir, appears in unexpurgated form for the first time—including the final, overwhelming chapter.

EXPOSED
$4.95/126-8

A volume of shorter Travis tales, each providing a unique glimpse of the horny gay male in his natural environment! Cops, college jocks, ancient Romans—even Sherlock Holmes and his loyal Watson—cruise these pages, fresh from the throbbing pen of one of our hottest authors.

BEAST OF BURDEN
$4.95/105-5

Five ferocious tales from this contemporary master. Innocents surrender to the brutal sexual mastery of their superiors, as taboos are shattered and replaced with the unwritten rules of masculine conquest. Intense, extreme—and totally Travis.

IN THE BLOOD
$5.95/283-3

Written when Travis had just begun to explore the true power of the erotic imagination, these stories laid the groundwork for later masterpieces. Among the many rewarding rarities included in this special volume: "In the Blood"—a heart-pounding descent into sexual vampirism.

THE FLESH FABLES
$4.95/243-4

One of Travis' best collections. The Flesh Fables includes "Blue Light," his most famous story, as well as other masterpieces that established him as the erotic writer to watch. And watch carefully, because Travis always buries a surprise somewhere beneath his scorching detail....

SLAVES OF THE EMPIRE
$4.95/3054-7

"A wonderful mythic tale. Set against the backdrop of the exotic and powerful Roman Empire, this wonderfully written novel explores the timeless questions of light and dark in male sexuality. The locale may be the ancient world, but these are the slaves and masters of our time...."   —John Preston

MASQUERADE BOOKS

BOB VICKERY

SKIN DEEP
$4.95/265-5
So many varied beauties no one will go away unsatisfied. No tantalizing morsel of manflesh is overlooked—or left unexplored! Beauty may be only skin deep, but a handful of beautiful skin is a tempting proposition.

JR

FRENCH QUARTER NIGHTS
$5.95/337-6
Sensual snapshots of the many places where men get down and dirty—from the steamy French Quarter to the steam room at the old Everard baths. These are nights you'll wish would go on forever....

TOM BACCHUS

RAHM
$5.95/315-5
The imagination of Tom Bacchus brings to life an extraordinary assortment of characters, from the Father of Us All to the cowpoke next door, the early gay literati to rude, queercore mosh rats. No one is better than Bacchus at staking out sexual territory with a swagger and a sly grin.

BONE
$4.95/177-2
Queer musings from the pen of one of today's hottest young talents. A fresh outlook on fleshly indulgence yields more than a few pleasant surprises. Horny Tom Bacchus maps out the tricking ground of a new generation.

KEY LINCOLN

SUBMISSION HOLDS
$4.95/266-3
A bright young talent unleashes his first collection of gay erotica. From tough to tender, the men between these covers stop at nothing to get what they want. These sweat-soaked tales show just how bad boys can really get.

CALDWELL/EIGHNER

QSFX2
$5.95/278-7
The wickedest, wildest, other-worldliest yarns from two master storytellers—Clay Caldwell and Lars Eighner. Both eroticists take a trip to the furthest reaches of the sexual imagination, sending back ten stories proving that as much as things change, one thing will always remain the same.... A special collections of stories, assembled especially for Badboy readers.

CLAY CALDWELL

JOCK STUDS
$6.50/472-0
A collection of Caldwell's scalding tales of pumped bodies and raging libidos. Swimmers, runners, football players... whatever your sport might be, there's a man waiting for you in these pages. Waiting to peel off that uniform and claim his reward for a game well-played....

ASK OL' BUDDY
$5.95/346-5
Set in the underground SM world, Caldwell takes you on a journey of discovery—where men initiate one another into the secrets of the rawest sexual realm of all. And when each stud's initiation is complete, he takes part in the training of another hungry soul...

STUD SHORTS
$5.95/320-1
"If anything, Caldwell's charm is more powerful, his nostalgia more poignant, the horniness he captures more sweetly, achingly acute than ever." —Aaron Travis
A new collection of this legend's latest sex-fiction. With his customary candor, Caldwell tells all about cops, cadets, truckers, farmboys (and many more) in these dirty jewels.

TAILPIPE TRUCKER
$5.95/296-5
Trucker porn! In prose as free and unvarnished as a cross-country highway, Caldwell tells the truth about Trag and Curly—two men hot for the feeling of sweaty manflesh. Together, they pick up—and turn out—a couple of thrill-seeking punks.

SERVICE, STUD
$5.95/336-8
Another look at the gay future. The setting is the Los Angeles of a distant future. Here the all-male populace is divided between the served and the servants—guaranteeing the erotic satisfaction of all involved.

QUEERS LIKE US
$4.95/262-0
"Caldwell at his most charming." —Aaron Travis
For years the name Clay Caldwell has been synonymous with the hottest, most finely crafted gay tales available. Queers Like Us is one of his best: the story of a randy mailman's trek through a landscape of willing, available studs.

ALL-STUD
$4.95/104-7
This classic, sex-soaked tale takes place under the watchful eye of Number Ten: an omniscient figure who has decreed unabashed promiscuity as the law of his all-male land. One stud challenges the social order, daring to fall in love.

MASQUERADE BOOKS

CLAY CALDWELL AND AARON TRAVIS

TAG TEAM STUDS
$6.50/465-8
Thrilling tales from these two legendary eroticists. The wrestling world will never seem the same, once you've made your way through this assortment of sweaty, virile studs. But you'd better be wary—should one catch you off guard, you just might spend the rest of the night pinned to the mat....

LARRY TOWNSEND

LEATHER AD: M
$5.95/380-5
The first of this two-part classic. John's curious about what goes on between the leatherclad men he's fantasized about. He takes out a personal ad, and starts a journey of self-discovery that will leave no part of his life unchanged. Soon he distinguishes himself as a true player, and begins the task of selecting a partner worthy of his talents.

LEATHER AD: S
$5.95/407-0
The tale continues—this time told from a Top's perspective. A simple ad generates many responses, and one man finds himself in the enviable position of putting these studly applicants through their paces....

BEWARE THE GOD WHO SMILES
$5.95/321-X
Two lusty young Americans are transported to ancient Egypt—where they are embroiled in regional warfare and taken as slaves by barbarians. The key to escape from brutal bondage lies in their own rampant libidos.

2069 TRILOGY
(This one-volume collection only $6.95)244-2
For the first time, this early science-fiction trilogy appears in one volume! Set in a future world, the 2069 Trilogy includes the tight plotting and shameless all-male sex pleasure that established him as one of gay erotica's first masters.

MIND MASTER
$4.95/209-4
Who better to explore the territory of erotic dominance than an author who helped define the genre—and knows that ultimate mastery always transcends the physical. Another unrelenting Townsend tale.

THE LONG LEATHER CORD
$4.95/201-9
Chuck's stepfather never lacks money or clandestine male visitors with whom he enacts intense sexual rituals. As Chuck comes to terms with his own desires, he begins to unravel the mystery behind his stepfather's secret life.

MAN SWORD
$4.95/188-8
The très gai tale of France's King Henri III, who was unimaginably spoiled by his mother—the infamous Catherine de Medici—and groomed from a young age to assume the throne of France. He encounters enough sexual schemers and politicos to alter one's picture of history forever!

THE FAUSTUS CONTRACT
$4.95/167-5
Two attractive young men desperately need $1000. Will do anything. Travel OK. Danger OK. Call anytime... Two cocky young hustlers get more than they bargained for in this story of lust and its discontents.

THE GAY ADVENTURES OF CAPTAIN GOOSE
$4.95/169-1
Hot young Jerome Gander is sentenced to serve aboard the H.M.S. Faerigold—a ship manned by the most hardened, unrepentant criminals. In no time, Gander becomes well-versed in the ways of horny men at sea, and the Faerigold becomes the most notorious vessel to ever set sail.

CHAINS
$4.95/158-6
Picking up street punks has always been risky, but in Larry Townsend's classic Chains, it sets off a string of events that must be read to be believed.

KISS OF LEATHER
$4.95/161-6
A look at the acts and attitudes of an earlier generation of gay leathermen, Kiss of Leather is full to bursting with the gritty, raw action that has distinguished Townsend's work for years. Sensual pain and pleasure mix in this tightly plotted tale.

RUN, LITTLE LEATHER BOY
$4.95/143-8
One young man's sexual awakening. A chronic underachiever, Wayne seems to be going nowhere fast. He finds himself bored with the everyday—and drawn to the masculine intensity of a dark and mysterious sexual underground, where he soon finds many goals worth pursuing....

RUN NO MORE
$4.95/152-7
The continuation of Larry Townsend's legendary Run, Little Leather Boy. This volume follows the further adventures of Townsend's leatherclad narrator as he travels every sexual byway available to the S/M male.

MASQUERADE BOOKS

THE SCORPIUS EQUATION
$4.95/119-5
The story of a man caught between the demands of two galactic empires. Our randy hero must match wits—and more—with the incredible forces that rule his world. One of gay erotica's first sci-fi sex tales—and still one of the best.

THE SEXUAL ADVENTURES OF SHERLOCK HOLMES
$4.95/3097-0
A scandalously sexy take on this legendary sleuth. "A Study in Scarlet" is transformed to expose Mrs. Hudson as a man in drag, the Diogenes Club as an S/M arena, and clues only the redoubtable—and very horny—Sherlock Holmes could piece together. A baffling tale of sex and mystery.

DONALD VINING

CABIN FEVER AND OTHER STORIES
$5.95/338-4
"Demonstrates the wisdom experience combined with insight and optimism can create."
                                        —*Bay Area Reporter*

Eighteen blistering stories in celebration of the most intimate of male bonding. Time after time, Donald Vining's men succumb to nature, and reaffirm both love and lust in modern gay life.

DEREK ADAMS

PRISONER OF DESIRE
$6.50/439-9
Scalding fiction from one of Badboy's most popular authors. The creator of horny P.I. Miles Diamond returns with this volume bursting with red-blooded, sweat-soaked excursions through the modern gay libido.

THE MARK OF THE WOLF
$5.95/361-9
The past comes back to haunt one well-off stud, whose unslakeable thirsts lead him into the arms of many men—and the midst of a mystery.

MY DOUBLE LIFE
$5.95/314-7
Every man leads a double life, dividing his hours between the mundanities of the day and the outrageous pursuits of the night. The creator of sexy P.I. Miles Diamond shines a little light on the wicked things men do when no one's looking.

HEAT WAVE
$4.95/159-4
"His body was draped in baggy clothes, but there was hardly any doubt that they covered anything less than perfection.... His slacks were cinched tight around a narrow waist, and the rise of flesh pushing against the thin fabric promised a firm, melon-shaped ass...."

MILES DIAMOND AND THE DEMON OF DEATH
$4.95/251-5
Derek Adams' gay gumshoe returns for further adventures. Miles always find himself in the stickiest situations—with any stud whose path he crosses! His adventures with "The Demon of Death" promise another carnal carnival.

THE ADVENTURES OF MILES DIAMOND
$4.95/118-7
Derek Adams' take on the classic American archetype of the hardboiled private eye. "The Case of the Missing Twin" promises to be a most rewarding case, packed as it is with randy studs. Miles sets about uncovering all as he tracks down the elusive and delectable Daniel Travis.

KELVIN BELIELE

IF THE SHOE FITS
$4.95/223-X
An essential and winning volume of tales exploring a world where randy boys can't help but do what comes naturally—as often as possible! Sweaty male bodies grapple in pleasure, proving the old adage: if the shoe fits, one might as well slip right in....

JAMES MEDLEY

THE REVOLUTIONARY & OTHER STORIES
$6.50/417-8
Billy, the son of the station chief of the American Embassy in Guatemala, is kidnapped and held for ransom. Frightened at first, Billy gradually develops an unimaginably close relationship with Juan, the revolutionary assigned to guard him.

HUCK AND BILLY
$4.95/245-0
Young love is always the sweetest, always the most sorrowful. Young lust, on the other hand, knows no bounds—and is often the hottest of one's life! Huck and Billy explore the desires that course through their young male bodies, determined to plumb the lusty depths of passion.

FLEDERMAUS

FLEDERFICTION: STORIES OF MEN AND TORTURE
$5.95/355-4
Fifteen blistering paeans to men and their suffering. Well knonw as a writer unafraid of exploring the nether reaches of pain and pleasure, Fledermaus here unleashes his most thrilling tales of punishment in this special volume designed with Badboy readers in mind.

BUY ANY 4 BOOKS & CHOOSE 1 ADDITIONAL BOOK, OF EQUAL OR LESSER VALUE, AS YOUR FREE GIFT

MASQUERADE BOOKS

VICTOR TERRY

MASTERS
$6.50/418-6

A powerhouse volume of boot-wearing, whip-wielding, bone-crunching bruisers who've got what it takes to make a grown man grovel. Between these covers lurk the most demanding of men—the imperious few to whom so many humbly offer themselves....

SM/SD
$6.50/406-2

Set around a South Dakota town called Prairie, these tales offer compelling evidence that the real rough stuff can still be found where men take what they want despite all rules.

WHiPs
$4.95/254-X

Cruising for a hot man? You'd better be, because one way or another, these WHiPs—officers of the Wyoming Highway Patrol—are gonna pull you over for a little impromptu interrogation....

MAX EXANDER

DEEDS OF THE NIGHT: TALES OF EROS AND PASSION
$5.95/348-1

MAXimum porn! Exander's a writer who's seen it all—and is more than happy to describe every inch of it in pulsating detail. A whirlwind tour of the hypermasculine libido.

LEATHERSEX
$4.95/210-8

Hard-hitting tales from merciless Max Exander. This time he focuses on the leatherclad lust that draws together only the most willing and talented of tops and bottoms—for an all-out orgy of limitless surrender and control....

MANSEX
$4.95/160-8

"Mark was the classic leatherman: a huge, dark stud in chaps, with a big black moustache, hairy chest and enormous muscles. Exactly the kind of men Todd liked—strong, hunky, masculine, ready to take control...."

TOM CAFFREY

TALES FROM THE MEN'S ROOM
$5.95/364-3

From shameless cops on the beat to shy studs on stage, Caffrey explores male lust at its most elemental and arousing. And if there's a lesson to be learned, it's that the Men's Room is less a place than a state of mind—one that every man finds himself in, day after day....

HITTING HOME
$4.95/222-1

Titillating and compelling, the stories in Hitting Home make a strong case for there being only one thing on a man's mind.

TORSTEN BARRING

GUY TRAYNOR
$6.50/414-3

Some call Guy Traynor a theatrical genius; others say he was a madman. All anyone knows for certain is that his productions were the result of blood, sweat and tears. Never have artists suffered so much for their craft!

PRISONERS OF TORQUEMADA
$5.95/252-3

Another volume sure to push you over the edge. How cruel is the "therapy" practiced at Casa Torquemada? Barring is just the writer to evoke such steamy sexual malevolence.

SHADOWMAN
$4.95/178-0

From spoiled Southern aristocrats to randy youths sowing wild oats at the local picture show, Barring's imagination works overtime in these blistering vignettes of homolust—past, present and future.

PETER THORNWELL
$4.95/149-7

Follow the exploits of Peter Thornwell as he goes from misspent youth to scandalous stardom, all thanks to an insatiable libido and love for the lash.

THE SWITCH
$4.95/3061-X

Sometimes a man needs a good whipping, and The Switch certainly makes a case! Packed with hot studs and unrelenting passions, these stories established Barring as a writer to be watched.

BERT McKENZIE

FRINGE BENEFITS
$5.95/354-6

From the pen of a widely published short story writer comes a volume of highly immodest tales. Not afraid of getting down and dirty, McKenzie produces some of today's most visceral sextales.

SONNY FORD

REUNION IN FLORENCE
$4.95/3070-9

Follow Adrian and Tristan an a sexual odyssey that takes in all ports known to ancient man. From lustful turks to insatiable Mamluks, these two have much more than their hands full, as they spread pleasure throughout the classical world!

ROGER HARMAN

FIRST PERSON
$4.95/179-9

A highly personal collection. Each story takes the form of a confessional—told by men who've got plenty to confess! From the "first time ever" to firsts of different kinds, First Person tells truths too hot to be purely fiction.

MASQUERADE BOOKS

J. A. GUERRA, ED.
SLOW BURN
$4.95/3042-3
Welcome to the Body Shoppe! Torsos get lean and hard, pecs widen, and stomachs ripple in these sexy stories of the power and perils of physical perfection.

DAVE KINNICK
SORRY I ASKED
$4.95/3090-3
Unexpurgated interviews with gay porn's rank and file. Get personal with the men behind (and under) the "stars," and discover the hot truth about the porn business.

SEAN MARTIN
SCRAPBOOK
$4.95/224-8
From the creator of Doc and Raider comes this hot collection of life's horniest moments—all involving studs sure to set your pulse racing! A brilliantly sexy volume.

CARO SOLES/STAN TAL, EDS.
BIZARRE DREAMS
$4.95/187-X
An anthology of stirring voices dedicated to exploring the dark side of human fantasy. Bizarre Dreams brings together the most talented practitioners of "dark fantasy," the most forbidden sexual realm of all.

CHRISTOPHER MORGAN
STEAM GAUGE
$6.50/473-9
This volume abounds in manly men doing what they do best—to, with, or for any hot stud who crosses their paths. Frequently published to acclaim in the gay press, Christopher Morgan puts a fresh, contemporary spin on the oldest of urges.
THE SPORTSMEN
$5.95/385-6
A collection of super-hot stories dedicated to the all-American athlete. Here are enough tales of carnal grand slams, sexy interceptions and highly personal bests to satisfy any hunger. These writers know just the type of guys that make up every red-blooded male's starting line-up....
MUSCLE BOUND
$4.95/3028-8
In the New York City bodybuilding scene, country boy Tommy joins forces with sexy Will Rodriguez in a battle of wits and biceps at the hottest gym in town, where the weak are bound and crushed by iron-pumping gods.

MICHAEL LOWENTHAL, ED.
THE BADBOY EROTIC LIBRARY VOLUME I
$4.95/190-X
Excerpts from A Secret Life, Imre, Sins of the Cities of the Plain, Teleny and others demonstrate the uncanny gift for portraying sex between men that led to many of these titles being banned.
THE BADBOY EROTIC LIBRARY VOLUME II
$4.95/211-6
This time, selections are taken from Mike and Me, Muscle Bound, Men at Work, Badboy Fantasies, and Slowburn.

ERIC BOYD
MIKE AND ME
$5.95/419-4
Mike joined the gym squad to bulk up on muscle. Little did he know he'd be turning on every sexy muscle jock in Minnesota! Hard bodies collide in a series of workouts designed to generate a whole lot more than rips and cuts.
MIKE AND THE MARINES
$6.50/497-6
Mike takes on America's most elite corps of studs—running into more than a few good men! Join in on the never-ending sexual escapades of this singularly lustful platoon!

ANONYMOUS
A SECRET LIFE
$4.95/3017-2
Meet Master Charles: only eighteen, and quite innocent, until his arrival at the Sir Percival's Royal Academy, where the daily lessons are supplemented with a crash course in pure sexual heat!
SINS OF THE CITIES OF THE PLAIN
$5.95/322-8
indulge yourself in the scorching memoirs of young man-about-town Jack Saul. Jack's positively sinful escapades grow wilder with every chapter!
IMRE
$4.95/3019-9
What fiery passions lay hidden behind Lieutenant Imre's emerald eyes? An extraordinary lost classic of obsession, gay erotic desire, and romance in a small European town on the eve of WWI.
TELENY
$4.95/3020-2
Often attributed to Oscar Wilde. A young man dedicates himself to a succession of forbidden pleasures, but instead finds love and tragedy when he becomes embroiled in a cult devoted to fulfilling only the very darkest of fantasies.

MASQUERADE BOOKS

HARD CANDY

BRAD GOOCH
THE GOLDEN AGE OF PROMISCUITY
$7.95/550-6

"Gooch's detailed descriptions and provocative observations make *The Golden Age of Promiscuity* the next best thing to taking a time-machine trip to grovel in the glorious '70s gutter."
—*San Francisco Chronicle*

"A serious limning of one man's (and, by extension, a generation's) search for identity." —*Time Out/NY*

KEVIN KILLIAN
ARCTIC SUMMER
$6.95/514-X

Acclaimed author Kevin Killian's latest novel examines the many secrets lying beneath the placid exterior of America in the 50s. With the story of Liam Reilly—a young gay man of considerable means and numerous secrets—Killian exposes the contradictions of the American Dream.

STAN LEVENTHAL
BARBIE IN BONDAGE
$6.95/415-1

Widely regarded as one of the most clear-eyed interpreters of big city gay male life, Leventhal here provides a series of explorations of love and desire between men.

SKYDIVING ON CHRISTOPHER STREET
$6.95/287-6

"Positively addictive." —Dennis Cooper

Aside from a hateful job, a hateful apartment, a hateful world and an increasingly hateful lover, life seems, well, all right for the protagonist of Stan Leventhal's latest novel. Having already lost most of his friends to AIDS, how could things get any worse? An insightful tale of contemporary urban gay life.

PATRICK MOORE
IOWA
$6.95/423-2

"Moore is the Tennessee Williams of the nineties—profound intimacy freed in a compelling narrative." —Karen Finley

"Fresh and shiny and relevant to our time. Iowa is full of terrific characters etched in acid-sharp prose, soaked through with just enough ambivalence to make it thoroughly romantic."
—Felice Picano

A stunning novel about one gay man's journey into adulthood, and the roads that bring him home again.

PAUL T. ROGERS
SAUL'S BOOK
$7.95/462-3

Winner of the Editors' Book Award

"Exudes an almost narcotic power.... A masterpiece."
—*Village Voice Literary Supplement*

"A first novel of considerable power... Sinbad the Sailor, thanks to the sympathetic imagination of Paul T. Rogers, speaks to us all." —*New York Times Book Review*

The story of a Times Square hustler called Sinbad the Sailor and Saul, a brilliant, self-destructive, alcoholic, thoroughly dominating character who may be the only love Sinbad will ever know. A stunning first novel—and an eerie epitaph for the author, who died tragically in the very milieu he portrayed in his fiction.

WALTER R. HOLLAND
THE MARCH
$6.95/429-1

Beginning on a hot summer night in 1980, *The March* revolves around a circle of young gay men, and the many others their lives touch. Over time, each character changes in unexpected ways; lives and loves come together and fall apart, as society itself is horribly altered by the onslaught of AIDS.

RED JORDAN AROBATEAU
LUCY AND MICKEY
$6.95/311-2

"A necessary reminder to all who blissfully—some may say ignorantly—ride the wave of lesbian chic into the mainstream." —Heather Findlay

The story of Mickey—an uncompromising butch—and her long affair with Lucy, the femme she loves.

DIRTY PICTURES
$5.95/345-7

"Red Jordan Arobateau is the Thomas Wolfe of lesbian literature... She's a natural—raw talent that is seething, passionate, hard, remarkable."
—Lillian Faderman, editor of *Chloe Plus Olivia*

Dirty Pictures is the story of a lonely butch tending bar—and the femme she finally calls her own.

DONALD VINING
A GAY DIARY
$8.95/451-8

"*A Gay Diary* is, unquestionably, the richest historical document of gay male life in the United States that I have ever encountered.... It illuminates a critical period in gay male American history." —*Body Politic*

Donald Vining's *Diary* portrays a long-vanished age and the lifestyle of a gay generation all too frequently forgotten.

MASQUERADE BOOKS

LARS EIGHNER
GAY COSMOS
$6.95/236-1

A title sure to appeal not only to Eighner's gay fans, but the many converts who first encountered his moving nonfiction work. Praised by the press, *Gay Cosmos* is an important contribution to the area of Gay and Lesbian Studies.

FELICE PICANO
THE LURE
$6.95/398-8

"The subject matter, plus the authenticity of Picano's research are, combined, explosive. Felice Picano is one hell of a writer."
—Stephen King

After witnessing a brutal murder, Noel is recruited by the police, to assist as a lure for the killer. Undercover, he moves deep into the freneticism of Manhattan's gay highlife—where he gradually becomes aware of the darker forces at work in his life. In addition to the mystery behind his mission, he begins to recognize changes: in his relationships with the men around him, in himself...

AMBIDEXTROUS
$6.95/275-2

"Makes us remember what it feels like to be a child..."
—*The Advocate*

Picano's first "memoir in the form of a novel" tells all: home life, school face-offs, the ingenuous sophistications of his first sexual steps. In three years' time, he's had his first gay fling—and is on his way to becoming the widely praised writer he is today.

MEN WHO LOVED ME
$6.95/274-4

"Zesty...spiked with adventure and romance...a distinguished and humorous portrait of a vanished age." —*Publishers Weekly*

In 1966, Picano abandoned New York, determined to find true love in Europe. Upon returning, he plunges into the city's thriving gay community of the 1970s.

WILLIAM TALSMAN
THE GAUDY IMAGE
$6.95/263-9

"To read *The Gaudy Image* now...it is to see first-hand the very issues of identity and positionality with which gay men were struggling in the decades before Stonewall. For what Talsman is dealing with...is the very question of how we conceive ourselves gay." —from the introduction by Michael Bronski

ROSEBUD
THE ROSEBUD READER
$5.95/319-8

Rosebud has contributed greatly to the burgeoning genre of lesbian erotica—to the point that our authors are among the hottest and most closely watched names in lesbian and gay publishing. Here are the finest moments from Rosebud's contemporary classics.

LESLIE CAMERON
WHISPER OF FANS
$6.50/542-5

"Just looking into her eyes, she felt that she knew a lot about this woman. She could see strength, boldness, a fresh sense of aliveness that rocked her to the core. In turn she felt open, revealed under the woman's gaze—all her secrets already told. No need of shame or artifice...." A fresh tale of passion between women, from one of lesbian erotica's up-and-coming authors.

RACHEL PEREZ
ODD WOMEN
$6.50/526-3

These women are sexy, smart, tough—some even say odd. But who cares, when their combined ass-ets are so sweet! An assortment of Sapphic sirens proves once and for all that comely ladies come best in pairs. One of our best-selling girl/girl titles.

RANDY TUROFF
LUST NEVER SLEEPS
$6.50/475-5

A rich volume of highly erotic, powerfully real fiction from the editor of *Lesbian Words*. Randy Turoff depicts a circle of modern women connected through the bonds of love, friendship, ambition, and lust with accuracy and compassion. Moving, tough, yet undeniably true, Turoff's stories create a stirring portrait of contemporary lesbian life.

RED JORDAN AROBATEAU
ROUGH TRADE
$6.50/470-4

Famous for her unflinching portrayal of lower-class dyke life and love, Arobateau outdoes herself with these tales of butch/femme affairs and unrelenting passions. Unapologetic and distinctly non-homogenized, *Rough Trade* is a must for all fans of challenging lesbian literature.

MASQUERADE BOOKS

BOYS NIGHT OUT
$6.50/463-1

Short fiction from this lesbian literary sensation. As always, Arobateau takes a good hard look at the lives of everyday women, noting well the struggles and triumphs each woman experiences.

ALISON TYLER
VENUS ONLINE
$6.50/521-2

Lovely Alexa spends her days in a boring bank job, saving her energies for her nocturnal pursuits. At night, Alexa goes online, living out virtual adventures that become more real with each session. Soon Alexa—aka Venus—feels her erotic imagination growing beyond anything she could have imagined.

DARK ROOM: AN ONLINE ADVENTURE
$6.50/455-0

Dani, a successful photographer, can't bring herself to face the death of her lover, Kate. Determined to keep the memory of her lover alive, Dani goes online under Kate's screen alias—and begins to uncover the truth behind the crime that has torn her world apart.

BLUE SKY SIDEWAYS & OTHER STORIES
$6.50/394-5

A variety of women, and their many breathtaking experiences with lovers, friends—and even the occasional sexy stranger. From blossoming young beauties to fearless vixens, Tyler finds the sexy pleasures of everyday life.

DIAL "L" FOR LOVELESS
$5.95/386-4

Meet Katrina Loveless—a private eye talented enough to give Sam Spade a run for his money. In her first case, Katrina investigates a murder implicating a host of society's darlings. Loveless untangles the mess—while working herself into a variety of highly compromising knots with the many lovelies who cross her path!

THE VIRGIN
$5.95/379-1

Veronica answers a personal ad in the "Women Seeking Women" category—and discovers a whole sensual world she never knew existed! And she never dreamed she'd be prized as a virgin all over again, by someone who would deflower her with a passion no man could ever show....

K. T. BUTLER
TOOLS OF THE TRADE
$5.95/420-8

A sparkling mix of lesbian erotica and humor. An encounter with ice cream, cappuccino and chocolate cake; an affair with a complete stranger; a pair of faulty handcuffs; and love on a drafting table. Seventeen tales.

LOVECHILD
GAG
$5.95/369-4

From New York's poetry scene comes this explosive volume of work from one of the bravest, most cutting young writers you'll ever encounter. The poems in Gag take on American hypocrisy with uncommon energy, and announce Lovechild as a writer of unforgettable rage.

ELIZABETH OLIVER
PAGAN DREAMS
$5.95/295-7

Cassidy and Samantha plan a vacation at a secluded bed-and-breakfast, hoping for a little personal time alone. Their hostess, however, has different plans. The lovers are plunged into a world of dungeons and pagan rites, as Anastasia steals Samantha for her own.

SUSAN ANDERS
CITY OF WOMEN
$5.95/375-9

Stories dedicated to women and the passions that draw them together. Designed strictly for the sensual pleasure of women, these tales are set to ignite flames of passion from coast to coast.

PINK CHAMPAGNE
$5.95/282-5

Tasty, torrid tales of butch/femme couplings. Tough as nails or soft as silk, these women seek out their antitheses, intent on working out the details of their own personal theory of difference.

LAURA ANTONIOU, EDITOR
LEATHERWOMEN
$4.95/3095-4

These fantasies, from the pens of new or emerging authors, break every rule imposed on women's fantasies. The hottest stories from some of today's most outrageous writers make this an unforgettable volume.

LEATHERWOMEN II
$4.95/229-9

Another groundbreaking volume of writing from women on the edge, sure to ignite libidinal flames in any reader. Leave taboos behind, because these Leatherwomen know no limits....

AARONA GRIFFIN
PASSAGE AND OTHER STORIES
$4.95/3057-1

An S/M romance. Lovely Nina is frightened by her lesbian passions, until she finds herself infatuated with a woman she spots at a local café. One night Nina follows her, and finds herself enmeshed in an endless maze leading to a world where women test the edges of sexuality and power. A bestselling title.

MASQUERADE BOOKS

BAD HABITS
$5.95/446-1
"Talk about passing the wet test!... If you like hot, lesbian erotica, run—don't walk—and pick up a copy of *Bad Habits*."
—*Lambda Book Report*

What does one do with a poorly trained slave? Break her of her bad habits, of course! An immediate favorite with women nationwide, and an incredible bestseller.

ANNABELLE BARKER
MOROCCO
$6.50/541-7
A luscious young woman stands to inherit a fortune—if she can only withstand the ministrations of her cruel guardian until her twentieth birthday. With two months left, Lila makes a bold bid for freedom, only to find that liberty has its own excruciating and delicious price....

A.L. REINE
DISTANT LOVE & OTHER STORIES
$4.95/3056-3
In the title story, Leah Michaels and her lover, Ranelle, have had four years of blissful, smoldering passion together. When Ranelle is out of town, Leah records an audio "Valentine:" a cassette filled with erotic reminiscences....

A RICHARD KASAK BOOK

SIMON LEVAY
ALBRICK'S GOLD
$20.95/518-2/Hardcover
From the man behind the controversial "gay brain" studies comes a chilling tale of medical experimentation run amok. LeVay—a lightning rod for controversy since the publication of *The Sexual Brain*—has fashioned a classic medical thriller from today's cutting-edge science.

SHAR REDNOUR, EDITOR
VIRGIN TERRITORY 2
$12.95/506-9
The follow-up volume to the groundbreaking *Virgin Territory*. Focusing on the many "firsts" of a woman's erotic life, *Virgin Territory 2* provides one of the sole outlets for serious discussion of the myriad possibilities available to and chosen by many contemporary lesbians.
VIRGIN TERRITORY
$12.95/457-7
An anthology of writing by women about their first-time erotic experiences with other women. From the ecstasies of awakening dykes to the sometimes awkward pleasures of sexual experimentation on the edge, each of these true stories reveals a different, radical perspective on one of the most traditional subjects around: virginity.

MICHAEL FORD, EDITOR
ONCE UPON A TIME:
Erotic Fairy Tales for Women
$12.95/449-6
How relevant to contemporary lesbians are the lessons of these age-old tales? Some of the biggest names in contemporary lesbian literature retell their favorite fairy tales, adding their own surprising—and sexy—twists. *Once Upon a Time* is sure to be one of contemporary lesbian literature's classic collections.
HAPPILY EVER AFTER:
Erotic Fairy Tales for Men
$12.95/450-X
A hefty volume of bedtime stories Mother Goose never thought to write down. Adapting some of childhood's most beloved tales for the adult gay reader, the contributors to *Happily Ever After* dig up the subtext of these hitherto "innocent" diversions—adding some surprises of their own along the way. Some of contemporary gay literature's biggest names are included in this special volume.

MICHAEL BRONSKI, ED.
TAKING LIBERTIES: Gay Men's Essays on Politics, Culture and Sex
$12.95/456-9
"Offers undeniable proof of a heady, sophisticated, diverse new culture of gay intellectual debate. I cannot recommend it too highly."
—Christopher Bram

A collection of some of the most divergent views on the state of contemporary gay male culture published in recent years. Michael Bronski here presents some of the community's foremost essayists weighing in on such slippery topics as outing, identity, pornography and much more.
FLASHPOINT: Gay Male
Sexual Writing
$12.95/424-0
A collection of the most provocative testaments to gay eros. Michael Bronski presents over twenty of the genre's best writers. Accompanied by Bronski's insightful analysis, each story illustrates the many approaches to sexuality used by today's gay writers. *Flashpoint* is sure to be one of the most talked about and influential volumes ever dedicated to the exploration of gay sexuality.

HEATHER FINDLAY, ED.
A MOVEMENT OF EROS:
25 Years of Lesbian Erotica
$12.95/421-6
Heather Findlay has assembled a roster of stellar talents, each represented by their best work. Tracing the course of the genre from its pre-Stonewall roots to its current renaissance, Findlay examines each piece, placing it within the context of lesbian community and politics.

MASQUERADE BOOKS

CHARLES HENRI FORD & PARKER TYLER
THE YOUNG AND EVIL
$12.95/431-3

"*The Young and Evil* creates [its] generation as *This Side of Paradise* by Fitzgerald created his generation."—Gertrude Stein
Originally published in 1933, *The Young and Evil* was an immediate sensation due to its unprecedented portrayal of young gay artists living in New York's notorious Greenwich Village. From drag balls to bohemian flats, these characters followed love and art wherever it led them—with a frankness that had the novel banned for many years.

BARRY HOFFMAN, EDITOR
THE BEST OF GAUNTLET
$12.95/202-7

Gauntlet has, with its semi-annual issues, always publishing the widest possible range of opinions, in the interest of challenging public opinion. The most provocative articles have been gathered by editor-in-chief Barry Hoffman, to make *The Best of Gauntlet* a riveting exploration of American society's limits.

MICHAEL ROWE
WRITING BELOW THE BELT: Conversations with Erotic Authors
$19.95/363-5

"An in-depth and enlightening tour of society's love/hate relationship with sex, morality, and censorship."
—*James White Review*

Journalist Michael Rowe interviewed the best erotic writers and presents the collected wisdom in *Writing Below the Belt*. Rowe speaks frankly with cult favorites such as Pat Califia, crossover success stories like John Preston, and up-and-comers Michael Lowenthal and Will Leber. A chronicle of the insights of this genre's most renowned practitioners.

LARRY TOWNSEND
ASK LARRY
$12.95/289-2

One of the leather community's most respected scribes here presents the best of his advice to leathermen. Starting just before the onslaught of AIDS, Townsend wrote the "Leather Notebook" column for *Drummer* magazine. Now, readers can avail themselves of Townsend's collected wisdom, as well as the author's contemporary commentary—a careful consideration of the way life has changed in the AIDS era. No man worth his leathers can afford to miss this volume of sage advice.

MICHAEL LASSELL
THE HARD WAY
$12.95/231-0

"Lassell is a master of the necessary word. In an age of tepid and whining verse, his bawdy and bittersweet songs are like a plunge in cold champagne."
—Paul Monette

The first collection of renowned gay writer Michael Lassell's poetry, fiction and essays. As much a chronicle of post-Stonewall gay life as a compendium of a remarkable writer's work.

AMARANTHA KNIGHT, ED.
LOVE BITES
$12.95/234-5

A volume of tales dedicated to legend's sexiest demon—the Vampire. Not only the finest collection of erotic horror available—but a virtual who's who of promising new talent. A must-read for fans of both the horror and erotic genres.

RANDY TUROFF, EDITOR
LESBIAN WORDS: State of the Art
$10.95/340-6

"This is a terrific book that should be on every thinking lesbian's bookshelf."
—Nisa Donnelly

One of the widest assortments of lesbian nonfiction writing in one revealing volume. Dorothy Allison, Jewelle Gomez, Judy Grahn, Eileen Myles, Robin Podolsky and many others are represented by some of their best work, looking at not only the current fashionability the media has brought to the lesbian "image," but considerations of the lesbian past via historical inquiry and personal recollections. A must for all interested in the state of the lesbian community.

ASSOTTO SAINT
SPELLS OF A VOODOO DOLL
$12.95/393-7

"Angelic and brazen."
—Jewelle Gomez

A fierce, spellbinding collection of the poetry, lyrics, essays and performance texts of Assotto Saint—one of the most important voices in the renaissance of black gay writing. Saint, aka Yves François Lubin, was the editor of two seminal anthologies: 1991 Lambda Literary Book Award winner, *The Road Before Us: 100 Gay Black Poets* and *Here to Dare: 10 Gay Black Poets*. He was also the author of two books of poetry, *Stations* and *Wishing for Wings*.

MASQUERADE BOOKS

WILLIAM CARNEY
THE REAL THING
$10.95/280-9

"Carney gives us a good look at the mores and lifestyle of the first generation of gay leathermen. A chilling mystery/romance novel as well."
—Pat Califia

With a new introduction by Michael Bronski. First published in 1968, this uncompromising story of American leathermen received instant acclaim. Out of print even while its legend grew, *The Real Thing* returns from exile more than twenty-five years after its initial release, detailing the attitudes and practices of an earlier generation of leathermen.

EURYDICE
F/32
$10.95/350-3

"It's wonderful to see a woman...celebrating her body and her sexuality by creating a fabulous and funny tale."
—Kathy Acker

With the story of Ela, Eurydice won the National Fiction competition sponsored by Fiction Collective Two and Illinois State University. A funny, disturbing quest for unity, *f/32* prompted Frederic Tuten to proclaim "almost any page... redeems us from the anemic writing and banalities we have endured in the past decade..."

CHEA VILLANUEVA
JESSIE'S SONG
$9.95/235-3

"It conjures up the strobe-light confusion and excitement of urban dyke life.... Read about these dykes and you'll love them."
—Rebecca Ripley

Based largely upon her own experience, Villanueva's work is remarkable for its frankness, and delightful in its iconoclasm. Unconcerned with political correctness, this writer has helped expand the boundaries of "serious" lesbian writing.

SAMUEL R. DELANY
THE MOTION OF LIGHT IN WATER
$12.95/133-0

"A very moving, intensely fascinating literary biography from an extraordinary writer...The artist as a young man and a memorable picture of an age." —William Gibson

Award-winning author Samuel R. Delany's autobiography covers the early years of one of science fiction's most important voices. *The Motion of Light in Water* follows Delany from his early marriage to the poet Marilyn Hacker, through the publication of his first, groundbreaking work. A self-portrait of one of today's most challenging writers.

THE MAD MAN
$23.95/193-4/hardcover

"What Delany has done here is take the ideas of the Marquis de Sade one step further, by filtering extreme and obsessive sexual behavior through the sieve of post-modern experience...."
—*Lambda Book Report*

"Delany develops an insightful dichotomy between [his protagonist]'s two worlds: the one of cerebral philosophy and dry academia, the other of heedless, 'impersonal' obsessive sexual extremism. When these worlds finally collide ... the novel achieves a surprisingly satisfying resolution...."
—*Publishers Weekly*

Delany's fascinating examination of human desire. For his thesis, graduate student John Marr researches the life and work of the brilliant Timothy Hasler: a philosopher whose career was cut tragically short over a decade earlier. Marr soon begins to believe that Hasler's death might hold some key to his own life as a gay man in the age of AIDS.

FELICE PICANO
DRYLAND'S END
$12.95/279-5

The science fiction debut of the highly acclaimed author of *Men Who Loved Me* and *Like People in History*. Set five thousand years in the future, *Dryland's End* takes place in a fabulous techno-empire ruled by intelligent, powerful women. While the Matriarchy has ruled for over two thousand years and altered human society—But is now unraveling. Military rivalries, religious fanaticism and economic competition threaten to destroy the mighty empire.

ROBERT PATRICK
TEMPLE SLAVE
$12.95/191-8

"You must read this book." —Quentin Crisp

"This is nothing less than the secret history of the most theatrical of theaters, the most bohemian of Americans and the most knowing of queens.... *Temple Slave* is also one of the best ways to learn what it was like to be fabulous, gay, theatrical and loved in a time at once more and less dangerous to gay life than our own." —*Genre*

The story of Greenwich Village and the beginnings of gay theater—told with the dazzling wit and stylistic derring-do for which Robert Patrick is justly famous. Though fictionalized, Patrick's debut novel stands as one of the most telling portraits of gay Greenwich Village in the years before Stonewall—and the many personalities who blazed new trails for American theater.

MASQUERADE BOOKS

GUILLERMO BOSCH
RAIN
$12.95/232-9
"Rain is a trip..." — Timothy Leary

The mysteries of Eros are played out against a background of uncommon deprivation. The tale begins on the 1,537th day of drought—when one man comes to know the true depths of thirst. In a quest to sate his hunger for some knowledge of the wide world, he is taken through a series of extraordinary, unearthly encounters that promise to change the course of civilization around him.

LAURA ANTONIOU, EDITOR
LOOKING FOR MR. PRESTON
$23.95/288-4
Edited by Laura Antoniou, *Looking for Mr. Preston* includes work by Lars Eighner, Pat Califia, Michael Bronski, Joan Nestle, and others who contributed interviews, essays and personal reminiscences of John Preston—a man whose career spanned the gay publishing industry. Preston was the author of over twenty books, and edited many more. Ten percent of the proceeds from sale of this book will go to the AIDS Project of Southern Maine, for which Preston served as President of the Board.

RUSS KICK
OUTPOSTS:
A Catalog of Rare and Disturbing Alternative Information
$18.95/0202-8
A huge, authoritative guide to some of the most bizarre publications available today! Rather than simply summarize the plethora of opinions crowding the American scene, Kick has tracked down and compiled reviews of work penned by political extremists, conspiracy theorists, hallucinogenic pathfinders, sexual explorers, and others. Each review is followed by ordering information for the many readers sure to want these publications for themselves.

CECILIA TAN, EDITOR
SM VISIONS: The Best of Circlet Press
$10.95/339-2
"Fabulous books! There's nothing else like them."
— Susie Bright,
Best American Erotica and *Herotica 3*

Circlet Press, devoted exclusively to the erotic science fiction and fantasy genre, is now represented by the best of its very best: *SM Visions*—one of the most thrilling and eye-opening rides through the erotic imagination ever published.

LUCY TAYLOR
UNNATURAL ACTS
$12.95/181-0
"A topnotch collection..." — *Science Fiction Chronicle*

Unnatural Acts plunges deep into the dark side of the psyche and brings to life a disturbing vision of erotic horror. Unrelenting angels and hungry gods play with souls and bodies in Taylor's murky cosmos: where heaven and hell are merely differences of perspective; where redemption and damnation lie behind the same shocking acts.

PAT CALIFIA
SENSUOUS MAGIC
$12.95/458-5
"Sensuous Magic is clear, succinct and engaging even for the reader for whom S/M isn't the sexual behavior of choice.... When she is writing about the dynamics of sex and the technical aspects of it, Califia is the Dr. Ruth of the alternative sexuality set...."* — *Lambda Book Report*

*"Pat Califia's *Sensuous Magic* is a friendly, non-threatening, helpful guide and resource... She captures the power of what it means to enter forbidden terrain, and to do so safely with someone else, and to explore the healing potential, spiritual aspects and the depth of S/M."*
— *Bay Area Reporter*

"Don't take a dangerous trip into the unknown—buy this book and know where you're going!" — *SKIN TWO*

DAVID MELTZER
THE AGENCY TRILOGY
$12.95/216-7
"...'The Agency' is clearly Meltzer's paradigm of society; a mindless machine of which we are all 'agents,' including those whom the machine supposedly serves...." — Norman Spinrad

The Agency explores issues of erotic dominance and submission with an immediacy and frankness previously unheard of in American literature, and presents a vision of an America consumed and dehumanized by a lust for power. Three volumes— *The Agency*, *The Agent*, *How Many Blocks in the Pile?*—are included in this one special volume.

MICHAEL PERKINS
THE GOOD PARTS: An Uncensored Guide to Literary Sexuality
$12.95/186-1
Michael Perkins, one of America's only critics to regularly scrutinize sexual literature, presents this unprecedented survey of sex as seen/written about in the pages of over 100 major fiction and nonfiction volumes from the past twenty years.

BUY ANY 4 BOOKS & CHOOSE 1 ADDITIONAL BOOK, OF EQUAL OR LESSER VALUE, AS YOUR FREE GIFT